TAKE MY BREATH AWAY

After the failure of her first marriage, romantic writer Emma has built a sheltered, secure life for herself and her four-year-old daughter. The last thing she needs on the horizon is a handsome stranger with an attractive smile. To make matters worse, her roof is leaking, money is tight and her ex-husband is taking a renewed interest in her life. Suddenly, Emma finds herself with as many complications to deal with as the tempestuous heroines in her romantic novels.

BETH JAMES

TAKE MY BREATH AWAY

Complete and Unabridged

LINFORD
Leicester

First published in Great Britain in 2010

First Linford Edition
published 2012

British Library CIP Data

James, Beth.
  Take my breath away. - -
  (Linford romance library)
  1. Love stories.
  2. Large type books.
  I. Title II. Series
  823.9'2–dc23

  ISBN 978–1–4448–0965–7

Published by
F. A. Thorpe (Publishing)
Anstey, Leicestershire

Set by Words & Graphics Ltd.
Anstey, Leicestershire
Printed and bound in Great Britain by
T. J. International Ltd., Padstow, Cornwall

This book is printed on acid-free paper

1

Oh, good! Someone was just pulling out of what looked like the only empty space in the municipal car park.

'Glory be.' Emma was, as usual, running late and she knew the post office would be on the point of closing.

'Mummy, he's holding out a ticket,' four year old Poppy said from the back seat.

'Who? What? Where?' Emma hated to be distracted whilst parking, but, yes, the driver of the BMW that had just vacated the space had opened his window and was offering her his ticket.

'Still has an hour,' he said. And was he tall, dark, and handsome and possessed of a devastatingly attractive smile? Unfortunately, no, he was not. He was sandy haired, middle aged, with rabbity teeth and furthermore, was accompanied by a very pleasant faced female companion — undoubtedly his wife.

'Thanks a lot,' Emma said, taking the proffered ticket with a smile. Transferring the square of paper to her teeth, she prepared to manoeuvre her old Nissan into the recently vacated space. Unfortunately parking had never been her forte.

Suddenly, almost silently, from the opposite direction, and in one swift move, a sleek black Volvo somehow slithered into the space — her space.

In dumbfounded disbelief Emma watched as a tall, loose-limbed figure of a man unfolded himself from the driver's seat and, with a long stride and an adjustment of his sunglasses, set off for the pay machine.

'Hey!' she yelled in fury once she'd managed to operate her gaping mouth. 'Hey . . . you've just pinched my space!'

The figure paused momentarily and then glanced unhurriedly over an uncaring shoulder.

'What?' he said.

'You heard,' Emma returned rudely. 'Look, the couple that just left gave me their ticket.' She shoved the soggy, tooth-marked square of paper through the window as proof.

The man laughed, showing off very white teeth and a deep dimple on his left cheek. She couldn't see his eyes from behind the dark glasses. For some obscure reason, she hoped they were small, squinty and deeply unattractive as he shrugged and spoke.

'Sorry — first come, first served.'

'But I was first,' Emma said, 'and you sneaked in while I wasn't looking. Furthermore, you drove against the one way arrow — that's against the law!' Ha! That would make him think.

The smile of amusement still hovering around his lips, he shrugged again.

'And you took someone else's ticket intending to use it and therefore defraud the council — I don't think they'd be too happy about that, do you?'

By now he'd really got under her skin. Who did he think he was, standing

3

there in his creased but undeniably good-quality jeans and linen shirt; his white teeth sparkling, his sunglasses trendy? A corner of her brain registered, too, that he wore no socks and his windswept hair was a shade too long. He looked every inch the film star on holiday. Not that she'd noticed, mind. Not that she'd noticed at all.

'Here, take the — the ticket.' She hissed against a tide of rage due partly because, whereas he looked the epitome of cool, she felt hot and sweaty. Also she was conscious that she was wearing the most faded of all her faded T-shirts, and was only too aware that her face was shiningly devoid of all make-up. 'You might as well take the ticket — to go with the parking space that you stole from me.'

'Hold on, weird woman,' the man said.

'I haven't got time to argue with you, you arrogant pig, I'm late already.' Emma let out the clutch and accelerated rather too fast, causing sparkling teeth to leap for his life. Smiling grimly into his surprised face, she speedily exited the car park.

'Mummy, what's weird and why were you rude to that man?' asked a determinedly interested small voice from behind her.

'Well, he was rude first,' Emma answered. 'Very, very rude and also extremely arrogant.'

'You called him a pig.'

'I know I called him a pig.'

'You told me you shouldn't call people names.'

'He wasn't a person. He was a bully. Anyway, some people deserve it . . . Taking my space like that. It's outrageous. I hope he gets a puncture.'

'That's not very nice, Mummy.'

'You needn't be so smug, either. It's your fault we're late . . . All that fuss about where Lucy Lamb was . . . Now, be quiet, sometimes there's a space by the library. Hooray, there is!' Trying not to feel guilty for being a bad-tempered mummy, Emma negotiated the available slot without incident and unfastened

Poppy, who was clutching Lucy Lamb, from her seat.

'Okay, now, if you're very good, after I've managed to get this lot posted, we might go and have a burger before we see Nanny.'

'Yes, please!' Poppy said. 'And can I have an ice-cream, too?'

'I'll see.'

'That's a yes, then,' Poppy said happily.

Taking her small daughter's hand, Emma sighed, briefly wondering just who was in charge here.

★   ★   ★

Chris completed his shopping in record time. A ready-cooked chicken, a bag of salad leaves, some crusty bread and a case of beer. That should do it. In fact, it was healthy eating. Take a gold star, Chris.

Yes, even if he did have an unfortunate habit of antagonising any reasonably attractive woman he happened to come across, he, Christopher Hemmings, knew how to eat healthily. Healthy eating was the one good legacy he'd been left by his ex-partner.

Fiona had been blonde, blue eyed and blindingly healthy. She had worshipped at the shrine of the body beautiful every day. Every minute of every day, actually. And she'd expected Chris to also worship. And he had. Well, for a while anyway — until the novelty of her washboard stomach and toned and tanned limbs and various other perfect body parts had begun to wear off. Then he'd found himself craving the odd portion of fish and chips and a girl with a lock of hair out of place, smudged mascara — no mascara, even — and a soft, curvy body to snuggle against. But not necessarily in that order.

He grew tired of the alarm going off at seven, of tripping over her dumbbells, of the reproach of her lycra-clad bottom setting off down the road as he waved goodbye. Nevertheless, when she'd finally hooked up with the fellow fitness fanatic she'd met at the gym, he was still surprised by the feelings of failure and guilt that had survived her departure from his flat and his life. All the same, he was relieved she'd taken her dumbbells with her.

So, for the past six months, he'd suited himself. He was a free agent and, boy, did it feel good. He could let his hair grow as long as he liked, he could neglect his fitness regime — yes, even the press-ups; wear clothes that were unironed, and he vowed he would never again go through the process of teeth bleaching for the sake of vanity. As for the suggested chest hair removal — and his eyes watered at the very thought — just forget it!

Swinging his supermarket bag, he turned the corner into the car park. Good job he'd just managed to grab the last space. No need to feel guilty just because some truly weird person with a small child had spotted it first. No need at all. Not his fault she'd been speaking to another driver through their open windows — what business was that of his? Absolutely none.

Okay, so he shouldn't have been driving 'in' the 'out' direction — he knew that was wrong. It was just the sort of perverse thing he'd been doing lately since the absence of a Fiona-the-fitness-fanatic from his life.

Pity the driver had been so pretty, it made him feel worse, somehow. Well, she hadn't been pretty, exactly. Arresting was more the word, with her flashing dark eyes, a few tendrils of dark, curly hair framing her intense face. She had attractive, silky, smooth-looking skin that had a rosy glow, too, not that hideous apricot, sprayed-on-all-over, matt finish that Fiona had sported. Just a natural sprinkling of freckles across her cheeks and at the soft rounded contour of her throat where it met with the scoop of a well-worn T-shirt.

Had he really been rude enough to earn the 'arrogant pig' she'd thrown at him? He owned that he probably had. Oh, well, just as well he hadn't really noticed her. Oh, no, she'd hardly registered on his radar at all.

★ ★ ★

By the time Emma arrived at her mother's cottage, she was feeling much better tempered. She always felt a little on the ratty side when she was about to post off a manuscript. Suddenly the idea that anyone could possibly consider her stories anything other than a trivial nonsense took such an iron grip on her that she had to force herself to package it up and say goodbye to it. It was almost as bad as leaving Poppy at nursery school for the first time. However, now it was done, it was done. No going back.

No point in worrying that maybe chapter six was a bit flat after the excitement of chapter five. No earthly reason in agonising over whether or not she'd managed to catch every incorrect spelling of phaeton as in phaeton carriage, which she'd only discovered had an 'e' in it near the end of the manuscript. It was posted — it was gone — and would shortly be winging its way across the Atlantic, leaving her with the delicious prospect of embarking on a new project. Emma felt a lightness of heart as she lifted Poppy from her car seat.

'Hi, gorgeous girl!' Monica stood at her cottage door smiling hugely as she always did when she set her eyes on Poppy. 'Would you like some lemonade? It's so hot today — my knickers are sticking to me.'

'I'm surprised you've got any on,' Emma said, laughing.

'Don't be ridiculous, of course I've got them on ... Although, I must confess, it's a tempting idea!'

Emma stooped to kiss her mother's cheek. Monica Hill was small, cuddly and a bit of a beatnik. This last fact had been the cause of some unease during Emma's teenage years, but with the passage of time, she'd grown to think of her mother rather as an eccentric, than someone trying to act the part of a hippy. For Monica may not conform to everyone's idea of the perfect parent, but where a grandparent was concerned, Emma knew that she could never find a better one for Poppy. Monica and Poppy loved one another fiercely and quite unreservedly.

'I like your toe nails,' Poppy said now.

'Do you, darling? I like yours, too.'

'Will you paint mine blue to match yours?'

'Of course I will, darling.'

Oh, well, out with the nail polish remover before Gavin's promised visit, Emma thought.

With a flurry of her trailing, ethnic skirt, Monica led the way inside the cool of the house, and straight through to the small garden behind. There, under a pergola adorned by a wisteria that had finished flowering, but now provided some much needed shade, was a low-slung hammock and a table containing a pitcher of lemonade and three glasses.

'I'll just get a couple of chairs,' Monica said. 'I expect Poppy will commandeer the hammock.'

'What does comman . . . What does that mean?' Poppy asked, settling herself comfortably in the hammock.

'What you're doing right now. Taking over the hammock before asking — you cheeky thing.'

'You don't mind.' Poppy laughed delightedly at her grandmother.

'Of course I don't mind, gorgeous girl.'

Emma sank down in her chair and accepted the lemonade.

'Have you eaten?' Monica asked.

'Yes, thanks, Mum. We've had a burger and ice-cream. Well, salad, too. Not all together on the same plate, you understand. And don't you dare look like that. You used to let me have burgers now and then'

'Who me? I wouldn't say a word . . . Is that your book all finished then?'

'Yep. I eventually sent it off in the post today.' Emma's relief was evident

'What's the next one going to be about?'

Emma wrinkled her nose. 'Well, it was going to be about smugglers . . . '

'But . . . ?'

'Can't afford to go to Cornwall to do the research. Well, I could if it weren't for the roof.'

'The roof?'

'I need a new one.'

Monica thought for a moment. 'I suppose asking Gavin . . . ?'

'Is out of the question? Yes, it is . . . Oh, he'd happily pay. But it would be one more thing . . . Well, you know . . . '

Poppy wriggled her way to the edge of the hammock and carefully eased her feet to the flagstones, then she danced across the garden to sit at the edge of the fairy grotto she had helped Monica to make, there to embark on a conversation with her imaginary fairy friend.

'Well, if he wouldn't mind ... ' Monica started tentatively.

'No, Mum,' Emma said firmly. 'Gavin does quite enough for us.'

'Well, he is Poppy's father.'

'I know, and he provides for her more than adequately, you know he does. But the house is mine and even though his mother left it to me specifically, for Poppy and me to live in, well, I still feel a bit guilty about it and that I should at least be able to maintain it myself.'

'Look, she didn't realise the roof would need redoing. She left you the house because she was upset when Gavin walked out on you. For goodness sake, she left him the flat in London, goodness knows what that's worth!'

'That's not the point! And, anyway, Gavin didn't walk out — I really threw him out.'

Monica looked at her daughter's mulish expression.

'Well, darling, what exactly *is* the point?' she asked gently.

'I'd just rather not feel beholden to

Gavin at the moment — that's all.'

For a long moment Monica said nothing.

'Oh, all right. If you must know, we had this really weird conversation all about relationships and how he wanted to play a larger part in Poppy's life. You know all that stuff he comes out with from time to time.'

'So?'

'So. He's playing a game, Mum. You know what he's like. He comes back exhausted from whatever war-torn country he's been reporting from, he looks at Poppy and he thinks: my goodness she's growing up and I'm missing it. He then persuades himself that he can change, that he doesn't need the constant excitement, that he could settle down again here, that he would be happy with just one woman in his life — me. And then . . . '

'And then?'

Emma shrugged. 'It's a no-no. We'd go through the whole charade again. And I'm not going there. Poppy and I do fine. Heaven knows he's always been more of an uncle figure than father figure anyway . . . She's hardly noticed the difference since he's gone and I'd like to keep it that way.'

Monica refrained from comment.

'No,' Emma went on, warming to her theme. 'He's welcome to dip in and out of our lives, now and then: of course he is — when the mood takes him. But he's not going to stay with us, and he's certainly not going to share my bed. He's not going to become a large part of our lives just to disappear as soon as something more interesting comes along. He's not going to do that to me again and he's certainly not going to do it to Poppy.'

Emma watched as Poppy gathered some fallen rose petals into her skirt and walked carefully towards her. 'I'm going to make you thome thent Nanny,' she said.

'You'll need some water then,' said Monica. 'And while we're at it we'll fetch that nail varnish. Now do you want the blue? I've got a rather fetching shade of purple; or how about yellow? And when you say 'scent' darling, you start off with your tongue behind your teeth, not between them, like this.' Stooping down Monica demonstrated. 'Sss. D'you think you can do that gorgeous girl?'

'Yes Nanny,' Poppy said, screwing up her face in concentration. 'Thcent!'

'Oh, that's getting really good. We'll have to think of a name for it next, won't we? The rose is called Peace. Shall we call it Peaceful Aroma?'

'No. I'd like to call it Thmelly Petal Thcent.'

Emma took a long drink from her glass. They were fine. The three of them. Just fine. Three girls together.

Who needed men?

2

Emma stared at the blank computer screen in front of her. She'd only been to Cornwall once in her life and that was when she was six. The few dim memories she had were of rain and cliffs, winding roads and hedges she couldn't see over.

She sighed. Why on earth had she decided to set her latest novel in Cornwall, when it was a place she knew little or nothing about? Because, she reminded herself, she'd had every intention of taking a holiday there with Poppy theorising that, whilst her daughter played on its sunny beaches, she'd lie back in the sun and let the Cornish atmosphere furnish her imagination. She'd counted on soaking up the rugged, smuggling history of the county. Pretty soon she would have been able to see and describe the houses her characters lived in, the craggy countryside around them, hear the way they spoke, conjure up their experiences and capture it all on paper. But now, what with the leaking roof, there was no way a holiday in Cornwall was going to happen.

The internet, of course, had been helpful. She'd borrowed from the local library, too, but somehow Emma knew that if she was to do justice to her story, and satisfy an American market that just loved a Regency romp set in fascinating old England, she needed a deeper geographical and historical knowledge of the area.

She sighed again. Meanwhile, the sun outside was shining, just beckoning her to enjoy the day. Normally she would give in, shut down the computer and take instead a large exercise book, sit under the shade of the pear tree and jot down a rough outline of the plot.

Only trouble was, she'd tried that yesterday. The resulting paltry three pages were now in the recycling bin.

Although, the day hadn't been completely wasted, at least she'd cut back the lilac, which had needed doing all summer, and Poppy and she had had an impromptu picnic of some late wild strawberries. But today Gavin had collected Poppy at ten, promising to bring her back at six and Emma knew she really must make the most of the resulting uninterrupted time and get on with the romance.

The hero was no problem. She'd had his physical appearance crystal clear for the last three days. Ever since the Parking Pig had pinched her car place, in fact. Her hero was tall and rangy, with an ironic lift to his eyebrow and a laconic way of speech, which contrasted well with her heroine's inability to stop talking for more than a second at a time. The appearance of her heroine however, she was having more trouble with. Should she make her small, red haired, freckled and feisty, or tall, dark, curvy and inclined to be bossy — rather like herself in fact?

Creating a new page headed *Story-line*, Emma left her list of characters for a moment and concentrated on the half formed plot she'd had in her mind since halfway through the last book. Within minutes, her hero, Hugo Trevellian, was striding across the page and odd scraps of dialogue were being inserted into what should have been only a basic outline to the story. But Hugo Trevellian, in spite of his speech always being cryptic, just would not keep quiet.

Lunchtime came and went. Emma's fingers fairly flew over the keyboard. She stopped and made coffee, but pored over a map of Cornwall while she did so. She was worried about time spans. Anxious about the viability, in Regency times, of crossing Cornwall from one coast line to the other. It was all very well calculating the distance, but Cornwall was rugged, the terrain very different from her native north Essex, and she didn't want to keep stopping in order to check facts and figures.

Knowing she'd have to spend more precious time on the internet, she sighed and went back to the computer.

Three hours later, ignoring the odd rumblings of her stomach, she was still surfing the internet, deeply involved in researching Mullion Cove, reportedly one of Cornwall's busiest smuggling centres in the eighteenth and nine-teenth centuries. But she was becoming more and more dubious about setting her story in this location.

There was a thump on the back door.

'Hi, there, any one around?'

Emma gave a gasp and checked her watch. It was quarter past six, no wonder she was hungry. She turned round to find Gavin and Poppy both framed in the doorway.

'Mummy, Daddy took me on the beach and we went on the pier and I had an ice-cream but then the top dropped off right on the pavement but Daddy managed to save thome tho it wasn't really dirty and we shared it.'

'Great,' Emma said as Poppy hugged at her hip, wiping her sticky face on her denim skirt in the process. 'So you had a good time, then?'

'Exthellent.'

'Excellent,' confirmed Gavin from where he was lounging against the kitchen table.

Emma ran a hand over her hair and straightened her skirt, wondering why it was that even though she was so totally over Gavin, he still had the ability to make her feel like the harassed housewife she undoubtedly was.

'Would you like some tea?' she asked now because it seemed the polite thing to do.

'Not particularly, but I could kill a gin and tonic.'

'I might be able to produce a white wine, but I'm afraid I'm out of gin.'

For a moment Gavin held her gaze. He looked older than his 40 years, his hair was thinning and he was a bit too much on the slim side, but even so Emma had to admit that he was still a highly attractive man. There was something about this slightly tired smile, about the way he pulled at one earlobe just before he asked a question that gave him a charm he was totally unaware of. He was pulling at his ear lobe now.

'How about I take you both for a bite to eat? Poppy and I had an early lunch, she didn't eat very much and I can see you haven't thought about food yet . . . So come on, why don't we?'

'Oh, yeth, come on, Mummy. Can we go to the place with the slide?'

Emma weakened.

'That's not a bad idea,' she said. 'It's the White Hart just outside the village,' she explained to Gavin. 'New people have moved in and they've put a swing and a slide in the pub garden.'

'Sounds good,' Gavin said.

★　★　★

And, Emma thought, an hour later, *it was good*. In a clean dress and with her hair freshly combed, Poppy sat quietly next to her, eating her chicken nuggets and chips with dainty fingers.

In the relaxed atmosphere of the pub, Emma had unwound a little and realised that, contrary to her expectations, it didn't feel odd to be sitting here with her ex-husband and daughter. In fact, it felt — well, good.

Gavin, when he put himself out, could be a good listener. In spite of his highly pressurised job of reporting from a trouble spot or, more often than not, a war zone, he wasn't above concerning himself with her domestic arrangements and the general trivia of her life. In fact, she had to remind herself, he was far more interested and caring now, than he ever was during their marriage. She wondered for a moment why that was.

She'd told him about cutting the lilac, about taking Poppy swimming and how she could float on her back now with just a small circle of screwed up face showing.

'How's your life going?' she asked

eventually, when she felt he'd been patient enough.

Gavin rubbed a tired hand across his eyes.

'Oh, as pressurised as ever.'

No new girlfriend, then, Emma thought. Although with Gavin you could never tell. He was always cagey about anyone new in his life despite having every right to have a new relationship now.

'But you love it. Your work, I mean, you know you do.'

'A love-hate relationship, I think you could call it.' He gave a half laugh. 'When I'm out there working and I ever get the time to think, I think of home. I think of here, even though I realise that it's not my home anymore, and I know that's my own fault and nobody else's . . . But then when I am here, after a few days, I'm restless and I want to be back there, working . . . It's just the way I am.'

'Yes,' Emma said, slightly surprised at exactly how accurately she'd summed

Gavin up to her mother just days before.

'So. How's the latest bodice ripper?'

'Excuse me? I think you mean historical romance.'

'That would be it.'

'Struggling a bit with the location, actually.' Emma pulled a face

'Oh?' Gavin looked at his empty glass. 'Hang on a minute, I'll get us another drink, and you can tell me all about it.'

'Oh, I don't know . . . We ought to go. Poppy's dead on her feet.'

'No, I'm not. It's really *weird* you should say that. I'm not tired,' Poppy said, yawning widely.

Emma looked at her small daughter, her face flushed, struggling to keep awake. How often was it that she ever got to go out with both her parents? She felt a twinge of guilt. This evening, the three of them together — something most other children took for granted — was probably special to Poppy. Why shouldn't Emma allow the

feeling to prolong itself?

'Okay, then. 'Weird' is the new word of the moment, in case you're wondering. Can you make mine a coffee?'

By the time Gavin came back with the drinks, Poppy was asleep with Lucy lamb clasped in her arms, and her head in Emma's lap.

'She couldn't make it, I'm afraid.'

'She's so pretty,' Gavin said, staring at Poppy's sleeping face. 'She's like you — but she's not like you, if you know what I mean. I can't believe I've produced such a lovely daughter.'

'Oh, I think if you cast your mind back, you'll recall that I did the actual producing bit. And she's always lovely — when she's asleep.'

'She's been lovely all day. Only one small crisis when we thought we'd lost Lucy Lamb.'

'Only one? We usually have several of those in a day.'

'So, tell me about the bodice ripper.'

It was funny, Emma reflected, how she never minded talking about her books to Gavin. Because he was a professional journalist — as she had been when she met him, although not quite on his scale — he never poked fun at her stories. Instead, he recognised that she was trying to turn out a successful piece of work, a product, for sale — the very best that she could ever do.

'Well, for some strange, or *weird* as Poppy would say, reason, I decided to set the story in Cornwall, only to discover it was a bad decision because I don't know enough about the area.'

'Well, in that case why don't you just change it to another location then.'

'Can't.'

'Why not?'

'It's about smuggling.'

'So?'

'Well, Cornish coast — famous for it.'

'Change it to Essex.'

'Essex?'

'Of course Essex. Smugglers from Harwich to Tilbury, through all the seventeen hundreds — probably up to now. Loads of material you can use, right on your doorstep.'

'Oh.' Now why on earth hadn't she thought of that? 'I'll have to have a bit of a rethink, then. But, actually, that sounds like a good idea . . . '

'Happy to oblige. Oh and another thing. I know of a local historian, by name anyway; I've never actually met him. He's done a bit of television work, written a few books on local history and he quite often gives lectures. I'll email him, see if I can find out if he has anything planned. I'm sure he could give you an idea for how things were back in the eighteenth century, what the coast line was like, all that kind of stuff.'

'Well, that would be great. Thanks.'

Gavin emptied his glass. Emma couldn't help noticing he'd had rather a lot to drink.

'Are you going to be okay driving?'

'Probably not.'

'You're not planning on going back to London tonight, are you? Because, if you are, you'll have to take the train. I'll drive you to the station. You must be over the limit, you can't possibly drive.'

Gavin smiled.

'Did I ever mention how bossy you are?'

'Several times, but seriously, Gavin . . .'

'I was hoping you'd offer me the sofa for the night.'

Emma stiffened.

'Oh, do me a favour. I'm not going to force myself upon you . . . You've been writing too many seduction scenes!'

A dubious grin spread across Emma's face. He was right, she was being ridiculous. The recent notion that Gavin was trying to worm his way back into her life on a more intimate basis was obviously way off track.

'Okay then,' she said reluctantly. 'But I want you gone early in the morning. I don't want Poppy to get too used to your being around.'

Gavin leaned over and easily scooped Poppy up into his arms.

'I suppose not,' he said sadly.

*   *   *

It had been a strange few days and Chris was feeling hungry. Hungry and restless. He wandered around his shop, picking things up and putting them down again. The stock was not moving fast. These days he only opened the shop three days a week and really he knew deep in his soul that the antique business was on the decline.

Luckily, he no longer relied on his shop to earn himself a living. He held onto it mainly because he'd inherited the business from his father and owned the premises. It was convenient to live in the upstairs flat, and he loved each and every one of the antiques he housed. But if it weren't for his television work, his column in an antiques magazine and a few fingers he had in other pies, he would be struggling to make a decent living. As it was, he somehow seemed to manage. Just.

He walked round the shop again, stopping to admire some hand blown glasses he'd managed to pick up for a song at a car boot sale. Drumming his fingers on the smooth oak of a small ladies' writing desk, he contemplated the possibility of going to the gym, and afterwards partaking of a healthy snack at their eatery, then quickly dismissed the idea on two counts. The first being that he might bump into Fiona, the fitness fanatic, and the second the remembrance that he'd cancelled his membership.

But dear, oh, dear, if this jittery feeling didn't quiet down, he'd have to do something totally out of character and go for a jog before he ate. Or, if not a jog, perhaps a walk? That was a better idea. A slow, sauntering walk, now that the heat of the day was over; a leisurely meander down through the village in the direction of the pub, perhaps? And who knew, he might meet a couple of male acquaintances, preferably ones without appendages of any kind and then they could spend a matey couple of hours talking cricket, or snooker —

anything, in fact, other than mentioning the female of the species.

It took him half an hour to get to the pub. He'd planned to take a short cut through one of the cornfields, but stuck instead to the narrow winding road because, for once, the traffic was really sparse and on such a fine evening he figured he was clearly visible.

He was just approaching the pub car park when a trio of figures came out of the shadowy interior. At the front was a tall slim man carrying a sleeping child, and a little behind him was a dark-haired attractive woman he recognised immediately. She wasn't looking his way. Instead she hitched her bag securely on to her shoulder, gave a low laugh at something her companion said, and gently removed a soft toy from the child's relaxed grip.

For a moment Chris stood stock-still. He felt out of breath, as though he'd been punched hard in the stomach. As though, at the very least, he'd suffered a mild heart attack.

Feeling like some kind of unsavoury voyeur, he stayed in the shadow of the trees, listening to his heart struggling for equilibrium. He watched as they settled themselves in the car and, with the woman driving, headed in the opposite direction from the way Chris had come. Then he let out a long expulsion of breath, shook his head impatiently and walked as briskly as his heartbeat would allow into the pub. He needed a drink, a drink and something to eat. That was it, he must be hungry. It couldn't have been the dark-haired, weird woman who took his breath away. All this healthy eating made you light-headed if you weren't careful, and you could start to imagine some pretty weird and wonderful emotions — all of which were absolutely ridiculous. If a man didn't watch out, he could end up barking mad from lack of food. Hadn't he just had proof of that?

Chris decided that the only cure could be a steak and ale pie with a generous helping of chips . . .

3

Despite hardly getting a wink of sleep, Emma woke early the following morning. For a moment she lay there marvelling the fact that for once she was awake before Poppy. Then memories of the evening before edged into her mind, quickly followed by the realisation that Gavin was probably still asleep on the sofa of the small living room of the cottage. She swung herself out of bed pretty quickly after registering that particular reality and washed and dressed in record time.

Cautiously she crept down the stairs and opened the living room door.

Gavin was asleep on his back and snoring slightly and Emma didn't have the heart to wake him. She tiptoed on through to the kitchen-diner and plugged in the kettle for coffee. She knew, of course, exactly how he liked it.

Black and strong, but not stewed. It was the only thing he verged on the fussy side about.

Her mother was right. It would be so easy to invite him back into their lives. After all, with his work schedule, they'd only ever see him for about one week in three. Poppy was old enough to understand that now. Poppy loved him. Gavin loved Poppy.

And perhaps Gavin had changed. Perhaps, despite being a Gemini, and a very typical one at that, perhaps he no longer needed two of everything. Two homes, the flat in London being one, this cottage in the country being the other. Although, of course, this home, had belonged to herself and Poppy since Gavin's mother's death. Maybe — although it needed a leap of faith to get past this one — maybe, he no longer required two women in his life. One of them usually a member of his crew or production team, and then herself, his wife, or ex-wife now, in the background.

For that was how it was still working. Only, since three years ago, when Emma eventually decided she could no longer bear the heartbreak of finding there was yet another woman on Gavin's scene and started divorce proceedings, Gavin no longer slept at the cottage.

Till last night. And, although nothing had happened, Emma was very determined that, too much to drink or not, that particular scenario would not be happening again. It was too unsettling. She was pretty sure she was no longer in love with Gavin, but she was only human, after all. Her bed had been empty for a long time, and writing about sensual, tempestuous heroes, who held no basis in fact — well not much anyway, apart from a passing physical resemblance to the sparkling-toothed parking pig — was hardly compensation for that.

Emma poured two mugs of coffee and peeped through the door. Gavin appeared not to have stirred. She gently edged a space on the small table next to his head, dislodging in the process his wallet, which fell to the floor with a thud.

Good, that might wake him up. But, no, Gavin snuffled slightly and the snoring ceased, but his eyes remained tight shut.

Bending to retrieve the wallet, which had opened in transit, Emma found herself staring at two photos beneath their plastic filmed protection. One was of Poppy, dark-haired, dimpled and smiling. The other was of a blonde, serious-looking woman who Emma didn't know and didn't want to know, but immediately disliked.

Carefully, she put the wallet back on the table, then she shook Gavin quite roughly by the shoulder.

'Come on, wake up. I've made your coffee. We agreed you'd go early, so you'd better get a wiggle on.'

'Eh? What?' Gavin looked startled and annoyingly boyish as he surfaced from sleep.

Emma hardened her heart.

'You can have a shower if you want, but the water won't be all that hot and, to be frank, I'd rather you didn't hang around too long.'

'Still as bossy as ever,' Gavin grumbled, reaching for the coffee.

'Just saying it as it is.'

★   ★   ★

Gavin left the cottage with a minimum of fuss, but the start of the car engine brought a sleepy eyed Poppy to the kitchen. Luckily she didn't realise what had woken her.

It wasn't till halfway through the morning that Poppy remembered having been out the evening before and, even then, she was more concerned with the fact that she hadn't been able to have a last go on the slide than that she hadn't had the chance to say goodbye to the father she saw so seldom.

So, thought Emma. *That was that*. Until the next time Gavin chose to put in an appearance. They could both manage without him perfectly well. The fact that Poppy didn't miss him when he was gone and was so well adjusted was proof of it.

She decided to give Hugo Trevellian a rest for a day, because if she were to change the Cornish scene to an Essex one, he'd have to be born again with a name to suit and her research of the area would have to start afresh. Besides, there was no nursery for Poppy today and Emma felt they should do things together.

So instead, she engaged on an untypical frenzy of housework. The windows needed cleaning and the duster and vacuum cleaner hadn't been out for ages. To make it more fun, she tied a handkerchief round Poppy's head and gave her a duster so she could help.

Together they made their way through the cottage, which was a typical country two-up, two-down affair with the addition at the back of a bathroom upstairs with a kitchen extension beneath. As she polished windows and sorted the muddle of Poppy's toy cupboard, however, Emma's brain went into overdrive. The photo of the serious looking blonde was never far from her mind, and the harder she polished, the more she worked up a righteous anger against all ex-husbands and hers in particular.

How dare he come here trying to weasel his way back into her affections, when all the time there was another woman on the scene? She'd given him the ideal opportunity to mention her, too, when she'd asked him what was happening in his life. How secretive could you get?

How dared he show concern over Poppy's lisp and nod in agreement, when she'd asked didn't he think it was getting better and wasn't he sure that it only came on now when she was very tired? And the novel, he'd advised her on the novel, too, and she'd lapped it up. Thought he was genuinely interested.

He'd even admired the fact that she

knew it was okay to prune the lilac now it had finished flowering and not wait until next spring as he'd have thought — as if he even cared what the garden looked like. And he'd actually had the audacity to suggest having the water-colour that had hung in the nook in the hall for as long as she could remember, valued, because his mother had always thought it might be a Cotman.

Yes, for someone who had a new girlfriend, Gavin was showing altogether too much interest in their lives, Emma decided, nonetheless stopping to examine the water colour landscape minutely before moving on with her dusting.

What with one thing and another it wasn't until after Poppy was in bed that she turned the computer on. She went straight to the internet and found 'libraries' in her favourites listing.

There, under forthcoming events, she saw that there was to be a lecture on the changing coastline of Essex to be given by a local historian in a week's time. *How very fortuitous*, she thought. Well, whether or not it was to be Gavin's acquaintance giving the talk, she judged it to be an event well worth attending.

She hummed to herself as she booked a ticket online. She knew her mum would look after Poppy even before she phoned her.

'Of course I will, darling,' Monica said. 'And I could have told you about Essex being famous for smuggling if you'd asked me. Just think of the pub names, that should've given you a clue.'

'Well, I knew myself at the back of my mind, but I'd got so set on Cornwall and Hugo Trevellian, I'd sort of tunnel visioned myself.'

'Nice of Gavin to help you, though.'

Emma bristled.

'Well, I'd hardly say telling me about a lecture qualifies as help.' She paused, uncertain whether to tell Monica about the new photo in Gavin's wallet. She took a deep breath. 'There's a new woman in his wallet.'

45

'Ah.'

'Yes, so don't go getting any ideas about us getting back together again, because it isn't going to happen.'

'Okay. Just so long as you keep things amicable.'

'Of course I will. Haven't I always? I just wish he'd stop pretending things could be anything other than as they are.' She paused. 'He stayed last night . . . Oh, don't get excited, only on the sofa. We took Poppy out for a meal, against my better judgement, I might add, and by the time I realised he was over the drink-drive limit, there was no other option . . . And that's what always seems to happen with Gavin. Give him an inch and he thinks he can carry on where he left off; have his cake and eat it.'

'Lots of men have mistresses, you know.'

Emma counted slowly to ten before she replied.

'I just can't believe you, Mother. How many times do I have to say it?

Fidelity is extremely important to me. I know what I can and can't live with. And I know you like Gavin; well, so do I, but not as a husband. The marriage is well and truly over.'

After Emma had rung off, she pictured her mother standing in her brightly-painted kitchen, possibly with a glass of wine in one hand and a stick of charcoal in the other. She'd probably frown for a moment or two, then shrug her shoulders, walk back to the large sheet of A2 paper she had taped to the wall and within seconds be back in her own world of copying another Degas nude with a towel.

Emma grinned, admitting to herself that she wouldn't have it any other way. They might be mother and daughter but they were both independent women and their lives were very different. Monica loved all things to do with art. She drew and painted, dyed cloth, made pots and fashioned rather strange patchwork quilts out of old clothes. She pottered around in her cottage with ancient jazz tunes emitting from an almost as ancient music centre playing softly in the background. But Emma never failed to find comfort in the fact that Monica was only ever a phone call away.

Back at her computer she found that an email had come through from Gavin, giving her the details of the Changing Coast Line of Essex lecture. She replied straight away.

Thanks for info on lecture. Actually had already found it, but thanks all the same. Em.

A minute later another email arrived.

Hope to see you and P two wks time. Perhaps I could stay over again. It was good to be with you both and go out together as a family. Gav

Emma decided a prompt reply wasn't necessary.

★   ★   ★

Chris whistled between his teeth as he collected his papers and books together.

He wondered how the evening would go. He'd had a shower and changed his T-shirt for a clean, but unironed and somewhat faded denim shirt, which matched his eyes exactly. His jeans were a designer model and dated from the days of Fiona, the fitness fanatic, but he didn't waste time brooding on that now. He had business to attend to. Pausing only briefly in order to bare his teeth into the mirror, and not wince too much at their still startling reflection, he let himself out of the flat door. Seconds later he was throwing his briefcase into the back of his second- or possibly third-hand Volvo and preparing to travel.

The lecture hall at the library was well known to him. It was a good size. Not so big that it was possible for empty seats to take on an embarrassingly dominant proportion, yet not small enough to appear mean or claustrophobic. From where he waited in the anti-room, he could hear that the attendance was large enough to be worthwhile. Chris counted himself fortunate because most of his lectures were well-attended. He always tried to make them interesting by introducing plenty of humour into what could otherwise be quite a dry subject.

The hands of his watch crept round to seven-thirty. Chris gave it three more minutes, time for people to settle and anticipate, then strode into the room, placed his notes, which he would probably not refer to, in the centre of the table. He turned and smiled at his audience.

'Good evening,' he said. 'My name is . . .'

His voice faltered, his mouth went dry, and it took a supreme effort of will for him to stay upright and smiling. For there, sitting smack in the centre of his audience, was the woman who had been popping into his thoughts with alarming regularity over the past week. The woman who had taken his breath away.

The rest of the room blurred a little

and became unimportant. Dimly, he realised he must pull himself together, carry on with his practised introduction. Although, just for a moment, he couldn't quite remember what it was he was meant to be lecturing on. And anyway, how on earth was he meant to talk about the changing coast line of Essex when there in front of him was the changing expression on the face of one of the most desirable women he'd ever set his eyes on. She was leaning slightly forward now; all her attention focused on him. The look on her face was slightly puzzled as though maybe she'd mistaken him for someone else, or as if she thought she might be dreaming.

Against his will, Chris finally managed to drag his eyes away.

'Good evening,' he started again, hoping his grin wasn't as inane as it felt. 'My name is Chris Hemmings. You thought I'd forgotten it for a moment, didn't you?'

A ripple of amusement spread

through the audience. *Good. Keep it going, Chris. You've done this a hundred times before. Just don't look at her and you'll be fine.*

4

Much to Emma's surprise, she found herself clapping enthusiastically at the end of the lecture. It had been a shock, of course it had, to find herself face to face with the Parking Pig, alias Hugo Trevellian, who had proved in reality to be Christopher Hemmings. But not so much of a shock that she hadn't taken a perverse pleasure in witnessing his discomfort on spotting her in the audience. She was delighted to note that his recognition of her had momentarily caused him to lose his stride, whereas she'd managed to cover her confusion pretty well, she thought, by presenting him with an expression of puzzled but slightly amused, recollection.

However it didn't take long for Emma to become totally enthralled in the wealth of information that Chris included in his evening's talk. He told how the Vikings had invaded the coast in a long series of plundering expeditions. How the hamlets of Lagenhoe, Fingringhoe and Wivenhoe, were all places named by the Vikings; how later the Normans made their mark, by sailing the Mersea river and founding villages such as Tolleshunt D'Arcy and Layer-de-la-Haye. His words painted a picture of the coast as a maze of mudflats, that shimmered like silk in the pure light.

He talked of tide washed islands with vegetation of sea lavender and green samphire, which used to be collected and eaten. He described the richness of the seemingly bleak landscape where wild duck, sheep and cattle grazed on the salt marshes. Emma sat mesmerised by his words, imagining long ships navigating the creeks and inlets where now modern yachts travelled. Briefly, he touched upon the birdlife: the gulls, curlews and redshanks likely to be spotted by anyone exploring this really fascinating stretch of coastline.

Halfway through the evening Chris apologised for running rather late, saying it was purely because he was so obsessed with his subject and tended to forget that not everyone else was so similarly afflicted.

'The interval will consequently be somewhat shorter than anticipated,' he went on. 'But please help yourselves to coffee.' He gestured towards a table by the door where the coffee had been laid out. 'After the break, if I haven't bored you to death by now, there'll be a brief slide show, then a question time.'

During the coffee break, Chris and the duty librarian, a rather prim looking lady in her early fifties, set up the slide show equipment and Chris disappeared in order to retrieve more notes from his car. Emma sipped at her coffee and wondered how Chris Hemmings the impassioned coastal expert could possibly be the same person as the dreaded Chris Hemmings the Parking Pig.

By the time the lecture was set to

continue, she found she really didn't care anyway because the lecture, which she had looked forward to as being a dull but necessary part of her research, had turned out to be interesting and entertaining beyond all possible expectations.

When the slide show was over, Emma realised she had quite a few questions she would have liked to put to Chris and found herself wishing, not for the first time, that she'd never set eyes on him before tonight. But knowing that she'd been remembered, and also that she had been quite inexcusably rude on the occasion of their first meeting, she held back, hoping that someone else might bring up the barely touched upon subject of smuggling.

But most of the questions put to Chris were to do with the geographical changes wrought in the coastline over time. Then there were queries about pollution — or lack of it, in recent years anyway — sweeping in from the Thames, which in turn could affect the fishing. Such was the ease with which Chris dealt with these subjects, that the questions turned into observations and well-controlled audience participated conversations.

Eventually, encouraged by the informality of the evening, Emma plucked up her courage and asked about the use of the coast by smugglers.

Chris repeated the question. 'Has the coast been used by smugglers? Funny you should ask that, I had an email from a guy just today asking how much smuggling figured in my talk tonight. I don't suppose he's here, is he — you two might have a lot in common?' Chris's blue eyes swept the room. 'No? Okay. Well, there were some very successful smuggling gangs operating up and down the coast for centuries. Their busiest time was from the early seventeen hundreds to the mid eighteen hundreds.'

'I suppose it was mainly spirits they brought in,' Emma said, thinking how well the time period would fit with her novel.

'Spirits, tobacco, muslins and silks, teas and even china, as well as anything unusual they thought there might be a market for. Customs offices were based at Harwich, Colchester and Maldon, but the smugglers were still highly successful.'

'It's not still going on, is it?'

Chris gave a lopsided grin.

'Perhaps you know the answer to that one? Bought any cheap ciggies in a pub recently?'

'I don't smoke.'

'I'm very glad to hear it.' Chris smiled at her for perhaps a little longer than necessary, and the depths in his twinkling blue eyes took her so completely by surprise that she almost gasped aloud. For a heart-stopping moment, it felt as though they were the only two people in the room.

She swallowed nervously and tore her eyes away, only looking back when the rest of the audience were included in the exchange.

'Oh, I've no doubt smuggling still

58

goes on,' he continued, but was he perhaps looking just a little unsettled? 'I've no personal experience, of course, far be it; but the proximity of France and the coastline itself must always lend itself to it. And, don't forget, as recently as nineteen-eighty-something-or-other, an aircraft landed at St Osyth carrying cannabis worth a million pounds!'

A few of the audience remembered the incident and immediately started on reminiscences of their own until, all too soon, the duty librarian stepped forward and thanked Chris for his most informative talk as the time for the lecture to end had well and truly come.

When the clapping died down, Emma found that, in addition to having two pages of notes, she had a strong reluctance to bid Chris Hemmings goodnight. After all, there was no real prospect of ever seeing him again, was there? She caught herself wondering whether to ask what other lectures he was planning, then reminded herself that he was, despite the good looks, terrific speaking abilities, pleasing manner and sparkling teeth, still the Parking Pig, and first impressions were usually the correct ones.

After returning her notebook into her bag and picking up her jacket, she glanced towards the table where Chris was collecting his things together. Only polite, after all, to thank him for an enjoyable lecture. No need to mention that she was writing a book or to dwell on the incident in the car park. No, certainly not. The incident in the car park was hardly worth referring to. Best ignore it; pretend it had never happened.

When she drew level with the table, she felt unaccountably nervous. Should she say, 'Thanks, I enjoyed that,' or maybe 'That was most informative, thank you,'?

As though sensing her presence, Chris looked up. 'Hi, there,' he said. 'We meet again ... Sorry about pinching your place in the car park. When was it? Must be a good couple of weeks ago now? I hope you have enjoyed this evening.'

'Oh, I have,' Emma said, feeling her face grow hot. 'And, well, about the car park thing — I expect I over-reacted. And, yes, I did enjoy the talk. You made it most interesting.'

'Nonsense, you didn't overreact, and you didn't actually manage to knock me down — although . . . ' He gave a sudden grin which made his face look more boyish and carefree. 'I'd say it was a pretty close call . . . I hate to think what you'd do if you were really mad!'

'I'm sorry,' Emma said, at the same time as registering that here she was, literally apologising — grovelling almost — when surely it was him who should be grovelling to her. And all because she'd discovered that his eyes, far from being small and squinty and deeply unattractive, as she'd, oh, so stupidly hoped, were blue and friendly and nearly as sparkling as his teeth. In fact, Chris Hemmings, expert on all things coastal, had turned out to be a real dish

— to look at, anyway. Not quite brooding enough to qualify for the part of Hugo Trevellian, the aristocratic, but cut-throat smuggler whose outward air of disdain covered a deep hurt in his past — but pretty damn attractive all the same.

Calm yourself Emma, she thought, *you're in real life now — not some historical romance.*

'I'd had a pig of a day, actually,' she said after a moment in which her mind's eye had dressed him in a flowing white linen shirt, tight, oh, so tight, pantaloons and black shinning top boots. 'And I thought the Post Office would close before I got there, but that's no excuse . . . I wasn't actually trying to run you down, though.'

With a final click Chris fastened his case. He grinned.

'Well, that's a comfort.'

Having dismantled the slide equipment, the duty librarian was now rearranging chairs. Almost without thinking, Emma picked up the nearest chair, placing it next to the others round a reading table.

'You don't have to do that,' Chris said. 'I'll give a hand in a minute.'

'I don't mind,' Emma said. 'I'm not in any rush, and I promise I won't break a chair over your head if you take my space.'

'It's very kind of you,' the duty librarian said, eyeing the two of them with interest. 'But there's probably something in the health and safety regulations forbidding you from helping.'

'Right. Okay, then, I'd better get going,' Emma decided.

'Right,' Chris said, looking a little disappointed. 'Oh, any reason in particular for your interest in smugglers? I hope you're not thinking of starting up in that line yourself, are you? I should advise against it myself. The rewards must be small compared to the enormous risks involved.'

Emma laughed. 'No, just some research I'm doing for a friend.'

'Oh, a friend?'

'Yes, a school teacher friend,' Emma lied. 'She's doing a project with her class.'

Chris raised his eyebrows. 'On smuggling?'

'Well, not just on smuggling,' Emma improvised wildly. 'On life in the eighteenth and early nineteenth centuries. How people made a living in this area. I thought smuggling might capture the interest of the boys.'

'Yes, you're probably right there . . . I've got more information at home on the Colchester Gang. Actually, some of the so-called aristocracy in the area were suspected of being involved in smuggling on a grand scale.'

Now this was right up Emma's street.

'Really,' she said. 'That does sound interesting.'

'Well, on a more legitimate level, there was the oyster trade, of course, and farming and fishing. The villages were mainly spinning and weaving villages, and four hundred years ago,

Braintree was a highly successful wool town. You can borrow a book I have about it if you like . . . Tell you what, give me your number and when I've had a root around at home I'll call you and you can either pick up the book and any other info I have from my shop, or maybe I could drop it round to you?'

Emma hitched at her bag strap to stop it from slipping from her shoulder. No need to think that just because he was being helpful, he fancied her in any way, of course not. He was probably only trying to atone for being a perfect pig the first time they met. Yes, that was what it was. Sure to be.

'Oh, well, okay, then . . . Um, my name's Emma, by the way . . . Right. If you're sure it's not too much bother.'

'Of course not. No bother at all. Anyway, I feel I owe you. After the parking thing, I mean . . . You know my shop, um, Emma?'

See, she'd known that would be it, he was saying sorry, that was all. She shook her head, wondering what on earth kind of shop Chris Hemmings would possibly own. She couldn't see him as owner of a men's outfitters or manager of a small general store.

'It's on Lexden Road,' Chris went on, his eyes resting on hers lingeringly. She was aghast to feel a tingle of excitement creep up her spine. Was it so long, that she thought every man who so much as noticed her was fanciable? She tried to concentrate on what he was saying. 'It's the small antiques shop, halfway between Little Lexden and the White Hart.'

'Oh, I know it. That's quite near where my mum lives.' For some reason she didn't add the fact that it was quite near to where she and Poppy lived, too. 'Okay, then, I'll give you my landline number.'

Chris punched the number into his mobile, and as she watched his long, tanned fingers, she gave an involuntary shiver imagining those same fingers entwined in hers.

'Great,' he said. 'I'm glad you enjoyed the talk. I saw you taking some notes.' He looked at her keenly. Emma felt slightly faint. 'You look like a bit of a yachting type.'

Emma laughed. 'Sorry, no. Chance would be a fine thing. I can't afford a yacht, let alone sail one.'

'Ah, well, I've got what could be described loosely as a yacht, I suppose, and I can sail her after a fashion. But she spends most of her time in dock. Needs a thorough overhaul, poor old girl. She's leaking like a sieve.'

There was another silence between them while Emma hooked her bag more firmly onto her shoulder again and Chris picked up a chair. Library lady was manfully struggling on alone in putting the room to rights.

'Well, I'll be going then,' Emma said eventually.

'Right. I'll call you!'

Yeah, Emma thought. *Right*!

5

It was more than a week later that Chris finally made a call to Emma's landline; a week during which Chris had put together some notes for a wetland wildlife documentary, and taken many photographs of wild fowl at dawn. On downloading them onto his computer, however, he decided the shots were too disappointingly mediocre to use for his pitch to an interested calendar manufacturer and that he would have to go out again when the skies were right.

Whistling gently through his teeth he, nonetheless, filed them under *Calendar Wetlands* before totting up the week's takings from the shop. They did not amount to very much. He could really do with finding a good piece of Morecroft or Clarice Cliff pottery at a car boot sale going for a song, but seeing as, despite good intentions, he didn't often actually manage to get to car boot sales, this would be difficult. Selling up was out of the question, but he had to admit to himself that the antiques business was becoming a bit of a tie.

When his father was alive and he ran the shop more or less as a hobby to prevent him going senile in his retirement, everything had been fine. Chris's father had had the second string to his bow of picture-framing and occasional picture restoration, which was his real love, and that had helped to make the business viable. But, for Chris, opening the shop and, between customers, working via computer link in the cramped space in the back premises three days a week, had become a duty to his father's memory rather than the pleasure it used to be. He felt the need now to be out and about more.

He wanted to spend more time back in his old life of working behind the scenes on history projects, or geo-graphical documentaries for television. It was freelance work and the financial rewards, although good, were fairly spasmodic, but opening a declining antique shop three days a week was not conducive to keeping a high profile within the media. Like it or not, networking was part of the game.

Not that Chris wanted to see his photo plastered on the front of any magazine. Far from it, he'd never wanted to be in the forefront of things, just a part of making sure that information on all things natural, things with a value — a worth, other than financial — was freely available to anyone with a television set. It was important to him to be instrumental in that. But, he argued with himself, his father's shop was worthwhile, too. It was practically a museum in itself, a memorial to good craftsmanship, to time spent lovingly in the preservation of a piece of porcelain, jewellery, or even weaponry, from another age. How could he give up on all that?

Over the last 18 months, he'd toyed with the idea of employing someone to keep an eye on the shop for maybe two of the three days, but he could see it might become complicated. Besides, would they love the shop as he loved it, treat it with the respect it deserved? After the Fiona experience, he doubted it.

No, he'd just have to limp on as he was, juggling the shop, the lectures, the writing and television projects altogether in the air, hoping all the time that he could dodge out of the way if a particularly heavy piece of furniture came hurtling out of the sky towards him.

He sat in the cramped workshop at the back of the shop now, and contemplated the small pile of books nestling next to his computer. It wasn't that he'd forgotten about his promise to deliver the books to Emma; more that he'd been putting it off.

This was because, although at the

time it had seemed quite natural to offer to help, afterwards he'd had to admit to himself that if she'd looked like the backend of a bus, and if he hadn't been very — extremely, actually — attracted to her, he wouldn't have bothered. Not that he minded being attracted to her, it was just that he knew, didn't he, that there was a small child and husband involved?

He sighed, he supposed his only course of action would be to call, hope she was out and leave the efficient and totally above board message on her answer machine that she could come and pick the books up on one of his 'open' days. The trouble was he didn't want to. What he wanted to do was call and say how about if he dropped the books round at a time convenient to herself? Then he'd hope the husband and child would be out of the way and, if they were, start on a campaign of seduction.

But he knew he wouldn't really do that. He had a few scruples left, and breaking up partnerships was one of them. Pity, though, there was something about her that set all his senses tingling.

Okay. Let's dial the number, then. See — it's easy. Nothing to it.

'Hello.' She sounded slightly breathless.

'Hi, it's Chris.'

She didn't pretend she didn't know him from Adam, even though it had been a week.

'Oh, hello, there.'

'Sorry I didn't call earlier. Things have been a bit frantic.'

'Oh, has there been a run on Chippendale suddenly or something?'

'Afraid I don't have any Chippendale. Edwardian, mahogany washstands are nearer the mark. No, I've had boring stuff to catch up on . . . ' That sounded terrible. 'But that's not what I've been doing,' he amended hurriedly in case she thought that she came way down the list after 'boring stuff'. 'No, I've been out with my camera. Wildlife shoots on the marshes. The light needs to be exactly right, you see, and it takes a lot of patience to get the right shots.'

'I can imagine,' Emma said. 'Did you take the photos you showed us all at the talk?'

'Yes, I did.'

'They were very good. Stunning — some of them.'

'Thank you,' Chris said, feeling ridiculously pleased.

'Did you find anything?'

'Eh?'

'About the smugglers.'

'Oh, yes. Yes, I did. Quite a lot. actually. When would it be convenient . . . '

'Well, I'm in right now . . . But, of course, you must be busy at the shop.'

'No, no,' Chris said quickly. 'I was planning on locking up shortly anyway. I'll pop the books round now.' Pop? Since when had he used the word 'pop'?

'Fine. I'll see you in a bit then.'

★   ★   ★

Emma looked wildly in the mirror. *Now, just stop it*, she told herself severely. *He's only coming round to lend you some books.* No, that was wrong — to lend her fictitious school-teacher friend some books. He wasn't interested in her, couldn't possibly be. If he'd been interested, as in wanting to know her better, he'd have rung long before this.

No, she was perfectly okay in her cut-off jeans and green T-shirt. All the same she applied a little mascara, but not lippy — that would be way too obvious. She ran her fingers through her dark hair, fluffing it up a little. It didn't really need a comb and anyway, she didn't know where one was.

Now, what did 'shortly' mean? Ten minutes? Fifteen? No reason to panic. She could just put the kettle on for tea, then, when he arrived, mention casually that she was just about to have a cup. Try to play it friendly but cool.

She heard a car pull up on the gravel beside the cottage, fled to the kitchen at the back and forced herself to take some deep breaths. The bell rang. Emma counted to ten before answering.

'Oh, hello, there; you were fast,' she said with a bright smile.

He was grinning at her in a way that made her wonder whether maybe she should have found that comb, and in his hand he carried an old cloth bag full of books. 'Come on in,' she invited. 'I'll unpack it and let you have the bag back.'

'That's okay' Chris said. 'It's not precious. No antique value. Keep them in the bag, I'll have it back when you've finished.'

There was no help for it — she took the bag. They were still facing each other across the doorstep.

'Would you like some tea? I was just making some — honestly,' she added, even while mentally telling herself how pathetic and desperate she must sound.

'Tea sounds good,' Chris said.

'Really? Well, you'd better come in, then.'

Hardly believing that she'd practically begged him to come in, Emma led the way through to the kitchen. Much better in the kitchen than the sitting-room. No question of where to sit in the kitchen. No sofa, just four upright stick chairs surrounding a pine bench table. Chris sat on one of the chairs.

'Nice cottage,' he said looking round at the small, but homely kitchen.

'Yes,' Emma said. 'We're very lucky.' She filled the kettle and turned it on, then busied herself with finding some milk, a couple of mugs and some chocolate biscuits.

'You haven't lived here that long, have you?' Chris asked. 'I seem to remember an older lady living here on her own. Mind you, I suppose that was a few years ago, now; she used to quite often ride a bike.'

'Yes, that would be my mother-in-law. When she died she left the cottage to us.'

'Oh, I see. I thought you weren't from round here.'

'Not originally, no. But it's my home now. My mum moved into a place up the road about ten years ago. She's an artist and she likes the light on this coast. Anyway, she became friendly with Gavin's mum.' She paused. 'Gavin is my ex-husband, by the way . . . I used to come down and stay with my mum for the odd weekend and, one day, Gavin was down here visiting his mum. Gavin does come from round here — he was born and bred here — he's a good north Essex boy.' Turning away from him, she splashed some milk in the mugs. Drat, she'd spilled some.

'And that's how I met Gavin. It was on the train, actually, and then we found that our mums were friends and we were both journalists, although obviously, he was a lot more successful than I was . . . ' She finished mopping up the milk and rinsed the cloth. 'And, well, here we are eight years, a four-year-old daughter and a divorce later . . . '

'Oh,' Chris said.

'I love it here,' Emma went on, aware that she was talking way too much and also that Chris was having a devastating effect on her — inside as well as outside. Quite apart from finding him physically attractive, it was so good to find that she'd been right at his lecture when she'd thought she quite liked him. She did, but it was more than 'quite'.

'At first, when we were first married, we lived in London. It's where the work is. But once Poppy was born, I grew to like it up here, especially when . . . Well, Gavin always worked away a lot. He's constantly reporting from trouble spots all over the world, really . . . ' Chris shifted in his seat as she spoke.

'Ah, that would be Gavin Fielding? I know him. Well, we've exchanged a few emails now and then, you know — research — and I've sometimes seen him on the box.'

The kettle boiled.

'Yep, that's him,' Emma said, filling the teapot with her back to him. 'It was probably him who emailed you about the smugglers. It was Gavin who advised me to come to your talk.'

'Ah,' Chris said again.

'Yes, we're on good terms,' Emma said, wondering if this was all too much information. 'We keep it that way because of Poppy.'

'Well, that's good.'

Emma shrugged.

'Not always easy, but worth it.' She stirred the tea and started pouring it. 'D'you take sugar?'

'No, no sugar . . . Take biscuits, though. 'Specially chocolate digestives.'

'My weakness, too,' Emma said, offering him the packet, then taking one for herself.

'I stuck some post-it notes on the smuggling pages,' Chris volunteered through a mouthful of biscuit.

'Oh, don't worry. I'll find what I want okay. I'm used to browsing at quite some speed.'

Chris looked puzzled. 'I was thinking of your friend.'

'Oh, my schoolteacher friend.'

Emma blushed a little. 'Ah, well. I do have a schoolteacher friend, but the information isn't really for her, it's for me.'

'So you're thinking of taking it up? Smuggling, I mean.'

Emma laughed, thinking that she mustn't make it too obvious that she liked him — liked his easy conversation, his light touch.

'No, too much of a coward . . . It's research for a book.'

'Wow! A novel?'

'Well, yes. I write for the American market. Swashbucklers, pirates, smugglers, beautiful young girls in distress — you know the sort of thing . . . '

'You mean you're actually published?' Chris said enthusiastically. 'That's great! I'm glad to be of assistance . . . But why didn't you tell me?'

Emma coloured. 'Sorry. I can't get used to admitting it. I used to be a journalist, you see, and all journalists say they'll write a novel, or secretly think they will. It's a bit of a standing joke.'

'Well, you're doing it, aren't you. You should be proud.'

'That's what Gavin says, but I regard it as a guilty secret. It's hardly Booker prize material. It's fun, though, and it helps pay the bills.'

'Hel-loo.'

Drat! Emma jumped and looked at her watch. 'That'll be my mum with Poppy. Mum's been looking after her for a couple of hours so I could get on with some writing.'

'And I went and spoiled all your plans.'

'Not at all,' Emma said as Poppy opened the kitchen door and stopped on the threshold at the sight of Chris sitting at the kitchen table. 'Hello Poppy poppet,' Emma continued smoothly. 'Have you had a good time with Nanny, then?'

'Yeth,' Poppy said, twisting Lucy Lamb's ear and eyeing Chris with extreme suspicion.

'Hi,' Monica said, squeezing herself through the gap between Poppy and the doorjam. 'Oh, hello,' she said to Chris. 'How are you? Have you sold my screen yet?'

'No, Monica, I'm waiting till you've managed to save up enough for it,' Chris replied, laughing.

Emma looked from one to the other of them.

'Well, it's pretty obvious I don't have to make any introductions here then,' she said.

'Your mum's one of my most valued customers,' Chris said.

'More like I'm your only customer,' Monica said. 'I keep telling you you'd have a few more if you were open more often.'

'Yeah, yeah, yeah,' Chris said good-naturedly. 'But, then, who'd photograph the birds? Who would keep the history of the area alive?'

With Monica and Poppy's arrival, they gravitated into the small sitting-room. Poppy started playing a complicated game involving Lucy lamb, a pair of knitting needles and a patchwork throw. Emma wasn't sure, but she thought the game might involve Lucy lamb undergoing some sort of life saving operation, because the knitting needles were being stuck into some extraordinary places. She wondered briefly whether Monica had been watching a medical drama on afternoon TV.

After Monica and Chris had exchanged a few reminisces about Chris's father and the heyday of the antiques business back in the eighties, Chris stood up to go.

'I'll see you out,' Emma offered hurriedly. 'Thanks for the books.'

'No problem,' Chris said, ducking to avoid a beam in the hall. 'Hey, what's this?'

He was looking at the 'maybe' Cotman.

'It came with the house,' Emma said. 'Why? D'you think it's worth something?' she added hopefully.

Chris bent closer.

'Could be,' he said. 'Lovely little painting.'

'We thought it might be a Cotman?' Emma said, feeling excited, now.

Chris laughed.

'You should be so lucky! I think your mother-in-law would have had it valued if that were the case . . . It's certainly his style, though, I should look after it if I were you.'

He turned away from the picture and took his car keys from his pocket.

'Well, thanks for the tea . . . I'll call you later see how you're getting on with the books — you know, yo-ho-ho and all that!'

'Okay, fine,' Emma said, searching her mind frantically for something — anything — to say that would ensure them meeting again soon. 'Thanks again,' she called as he started the car.

'Goodbye,' she said as his car disappeared down the road.

6

She could hear the steady drip, drip, drip even through a dream she was having about toasting marshmallows at a bonfire on the beach. The dream was so real she could almost smell the wood smoke and hear the suck and swell of the tide on the shingle beach. There were shadows behind her, possibly masking the entrance of a cave. That must be it; a cave full of moisture and the moisture was collecting of the roof and steadily dripping into a pool beneath.

Drip, drip, kerplonk. Drip, drip, kerplonk.

Emma stirred in her sleep, then sat up with a jerk. Drip, drip, kerplonk!

Oh, no! She looked out of the window. Oh, yes! It was raining, and it wasn't soft summer rain either. It was lashing it down as though it were the middle of December.

Luckily she'd had the forethought to leave the ladder propped up on the landing, not the safest of places, as Gavin had commented when he'd seen them, but handy in case of roof leak alert, which was something she hadn't bothered to explain at the time.

Warily, Emma eyed the ceiling. No sign of damp yet. She leapt into action and, within minutes, had the ladders balanced against the opening to the loft hatch, which was somewhat inconveniently positioned in the corner of her bedroom. She ran down the stairs for a spare ice-cream container of which, thanks to Poppy's partiality for ice-cream, she had plenty.

Right, it was up the ladder time. Trying not to think about spiders, the possibility of nesting squirrels or — please, no — rats! She pushed the loft hatch open, groped for the light switch and looked in alarm at the plastic ice-cream container she'd put there last time it rained, which was on the point of overflowing. Gingerly she inched it towards her and put the empty one in its place. Carrying the full one down the stepladder would be more of a challenge. Stupid to risk spilling it and staining the ceiling — nothing for it but another trip to the kitchen for a third container.

She cast an anxious eye around the rest of the loft. Thank goodness for that, there were no more wet patches that she could see in the subdued light. Just a moment. She could see a small patch of light coming from the corner by the front porch. The tile was loose, she'd spotted it from outside, but so far, although there was a drip in the outside porch, the dampness hadn't extended to the hall. Really she should fetch a torch and have a good look or the chances were she'd find herself worrying about it in the middle of the night.

Lightly, she ran down the stairs. Who needed an expensive exercise regime when she could have all this activity going on every time it rained?

A few minutes later, Emma had transferred half the water from the first brimming container and now had two ice-cream containers half full of water to carry down the ladder — or half empty, she supposed, depending upon which way you looked at it. Either way, it was tricky, very tricky. With a steadiness and grace she didn't know she possessed, she backed down the steps. Easy peasy, really. No need to get in a state about these little things sent to try us single mothers on, what seemed to be becoming, a regular basis.

As she emptied the water in the small bathroom, she heard Poppy talking to Lucy Lamb. It was still raining hard. Emma forgot all about the torch inspection of the loft, and just lined up the two containers ready for next time and went to say good morning to her daughter.

It wasn't until an hour l   when Poppy had been dressed   ak-fasted and was watching a   e

DVD, that Emma switched on her computer. There had been nothing remotely interesting in the post this morning — not even a rejection slip, so she might as well read her emails.

A moment later she was wishing that she hadn't.

Her American editor was sorry to advise her that her novel, set against the backdrop of the French Revolution as it was, could not be accepted at this time. Unfortunately it was too similar to another book, dealing with the storming of the Bastille, that had only recently been accepted.

Emma could hardly believe it. *But I sent her a rough outline*, she thought. *I told her it was set in Paris in 1789, how could anybody dealing in historical romance not know that was the date of the storming of the Bastille? An American editor*, she answered herself immediately, and how stupid was she herself, not to have made the setting of the story more clear. It was her own fault; she had no one to blame but herself. This was what came of becoming too complacent. But it meant six months work down the drain, not to mention the previous nine months when she'd been nursing the whole idea along in her brain.

Bit like a pregnancy, really, she thought to herself — only this time there was no actual birth at the end of it. No arrival by post of the first sample copies, no surprise as she looked to see whether her heroine on the front cover bore any resemblance to the one in her imagination. Keep it in proportion, Emma. A book is not a baby; nowhere in the same league as a baby. It's not the end of the world.

She read the email again. Her editor suggested that, unless Emma had another market in mind, she would sit on the novel for eighteen months or so before reconsidering. So that was the good news, she supposed. She allowed herself a small smile. That was at least the advantage of historical romance — it didn't date! She rattled off a quick email to the States, outlining the smuggler plot and asking for verification that there was not another 'smuggler' plot set in eighteenth-century Essex about to be accepted. Then she glanced at her watch, registering the time difference and that she'd have to wait till this evening at the earliest before she had a reply on that one. Meanwhile there was nothing for it; she would just have to battle on with 'smuggler' and hope!

All the same, the thought of the non-arrival of the French Revolution cheque was daunting, especially in the light of the leak that might at any moment appear in the hall ceiling where the porch met the slate roof. Not to mention the one in her own bedroom which she was managing to prevent staining the ceiling only by changing the plastic ice-cream containers in the loft on a regular basis — as in this morning's fiasco.

Emma put her head in her hands. It was at times like this that she really missed having a husband. The awful thing was that she knew she only had to pick up the phone, tell Gavin about the leak and she could have a roofer round in a matter of, if not minutes, then hours. Should she? Somehow she couldn't bring herself to do so. Perhaps if the leak had been in Poppy's bedroom, she would have done, but it wasn't, and anyway Emma was born to be independent and her own mother had never had anyone to call and sort things out for her — had she? Monica had had to battle on alone.

Emma sighed. She really hadn't wished for this sort of single parent life for Poppy. After her own 'no father' childhood, she'd wanted a conventional family life for her own daughter. She'd wanted her to know the comfort of a male at the head of the household. Instead it was just herself and Monica who made up Poppy's family. Although, there had been a hamster for a while. He was called William and so presumably was male — even Emma had to concede that a male hamster couldn't be considered a role model exactly.

Somehow she was no longer in the mood for writing, so she closed the computer. The rain was still streaming down the windows while Emma moved restlessly round the house performing everyday chores as she went. In a moment she'd be strict with herself, sit down at her computer and get some serious work done. She should be doing it right now because Poppy was silently watching the television and that wouldn't last for too long.

First, she'd just make the beds. Upstairs she went into Poppy's room; it smelled of Poppy when she was freshly bathed — sweet and powdery. It was a real girly room, a princess's paradise. Flying across one wall were fairies, painted by Monica; a castle fit for a princess in thc distance. The bed was covered with a gauze canopy that looked like butterfly wings, with curtains at the window to match. The room was everything that was pretty and Poppy loved it.

Occasionally Emma wondered whether or not it was the right thing to do to fill Poppy's head with such nonsense, then she reminded herself of how short a childhood really was and reasoned that why shouldn't her daughter believe in fairies for a while — where was the harm? Just as long as she didn't also believe in fairy princes who came along on their white chargers and rescued princesses from all of life's problems, including leaky roofs. No, she had to show Poppy that a woman alone could cope as well, if not better, than a woman with a man. There was no way she would call Gavin. Absolutely not.

She shut the door and progressed to her own room, which had been made considerably smaller by the addition of the ladder propped against the wall to give her immediate access to the loft. She glanced out of the window — it was still raining. Oh, well, she'd better get climbing before it overflowed again. She picked up the replacement empty ice-cream container and mounted the steps once more. 'Mummy, what are you doing?' Poppy's voice quavered from below.

'Mummy's trying to stop us from drowning,' Emma said, struggling to stop the water from tipping out of the flimsy container as she backed down the steps. 'Move out of the way, poppet, there's a sweetheart.'

Afterwards, Emma couldn't quite figure out how it had happened. One minute she was standing on the ladder holding the water in one hand and the metal of the step above her with the other, the next moment she was on the floor, nursing a bruised elbow and trying to comfort a sobbing Poppy who was soaking wet. Over the top of Poppy's head she contemplated her bed on which the upside-down container had emptied the bulk of the rainwater. It had, of course, landed dead centre.

'Why did you do that?' Poppy wailed indignantly between sobs. 'I'm all wet.'

'I didn't do it on purpose,' Emma

said, feeling like joining in the sobbing.

A hot shower with Poppy, and a cup of tea later, Emma phoned Gavin.

'Hello?' The voice belonged to the blonde with the serious expression, Emma just knew it did. She hung up, and with a grim expression on her face, dialled the roofer's number.

★ ★ ★

Chris couldn't concentrate. It must be the rain, he decided. It really was incessant. It was unsettling, too, especially after the heat of recent weeks. So far this morning he'd not even had one customer. Not even a browser. He should have been getting on with his proper work. His notes on Brightlingsea with its views across the Coine Estuary were already on computer, but he needed to vamp up the descriptions that went with his suggested calendar shots with a few exotic phrases.

He brought up the camera images on

screen yet again. *You're a genius Hemmings*, he told himself as he came to his most recent and almost perfect view of the opalescent mud flats in the estuary. Surely he could conjure up a poetic caption for this photograph. *Think Chris, think. How about, 'The tide slides stealthily in, like a silk stocking over a woman's thigh.'? No, perhaps not.* Although, that was exactly how Chris thought of it. One woman's thigh in particular, actually. A woman he had no business thinking about at all, let alone imagining the silkiness of her thighs.

He gave a sigh. Had he realised how difficult it would be to get her out of his mind, he would never have offered Emma the loan of his books. Having done so, he knew that if he didn't want to lose his books for ever he would have to see her at least one more time in order to get them back. And he really didn't want to.

She was too attractive, too nice, too interesting, too vulnerable, too recently divorced, and too near to him geo-graphically to be comfortable with when it all went wrong — as it was bound to.

Although, of course, he'd never set eyes on her until — was it only three weeks ago? A month? Something like that. Chris seemed to have lost track of time where she was concerned, and was only aware of the profound effect his knowing of her presence, her living in the near vicinity, had on him. Each time he got into his car in order to make a local journey, he wondered if he might catch a glimpse of her walking down a street with Poppy. It had got to the stage when every time he saw a dark-and curly-haired little girl, he automati-cally stared at the mother hoping it might be Emma.

In a small supermarket the other day he'd received some very suspicious looks from a man he later discovered to be with a shopping trolley pushing lady he'd been watching closely, and was quite positive was Emma, from behind.

On discovering his mistake he'd had to veer violently in the other direction to hide his discomfiture.

It didn't matter, either, how often he told himself he was a sad case, and that he really shouldn't pursue this because a) he'd already proved to himself, hadn't he, many times over, that he was no good at relationships? Also that b) this particular relationship was a no-no, because there was not only a child involved, but an ex-husband as well, and the fact that he seemed to be on good terms with Emma could prove tricky.

Chris scowled. So why should he be noble? What had got into him all of a sudden that he was putting other people's happiness before his own? Because it was three other people, he answered himself. Three other people who were all very pleasant people getting on with their very nice lives, they certainly didn't need him coming in on the scene and lousing it all up for them. Anyway, why on earth should someone as obviously lovely as Emma be remotely interested in him?

And right now, he needed to get back to work, to banish the beautiful and desirable Emma from his thoughts and return to calendar captions.

He worked for an undisturbed two hours and eventually felt he was getting the hang of it. Really, he could have been a poet, he fantasised. Not much money in it, of course, but the elation he felt when he got a line exactly right might make up for that. There was one line he was particularly pleased with to do with *lazy bees buzzing over hazy summer meadows* and another about *the call of the curlews breaking the silence of the summer sky.*

The Colne Estuary caption proved more troublesome, but in the end he lost the thigh reference, kept the silk, added 'smooth chocolate', and at last he was satisfied.

He pushed himself away from the computer and stretched like a cat. See, he told himself, *you managed a good two hours there without a thought of Emma entering your mind.*

His phone rang. It was his mobile, not the landline in the shop.

'Hello,' Emma said. 'At the risk of being a pain, I have another favour to ask of you . . . '

A ridiculous grin was overtaking the delighted surprise on Chris's face.

'Ask away,' he said softly.

7

The shop bell jangled as Emma pushed the door open. 'Can't stop,' she said as Chris came towards her with a delighted smile on his face. 'Poppy's fallen asleep in the car.'

Trying not to notice the disappointment in Chris's eyes, she thrust the cardboard box at him.

'There's the three of them there together. The one off the hall wall, and one — very similar — I found together with the one of the church. They're the two I've only just discovered up in the loft.'

'Wow,' Chris said. 'Cash in the attic, eh?'

Emma gave a nervous laugh.

'That would be, oh, so very welcome,' she said. 'The reason I was in the loft was because I've got not one, but two, as of this morning, leaks in the roof. This box was wedged up under the eaves; there's a slate that's dislodged right above it, but luckily the pictures didn't get wet . . . Anyway, as I said, Poppy's in the car.'

'Can't you bring her in?'

For a moment, Emma was tempted, but she shook her head.

'No, she's a real misery if she wakes up. Anyway, you must be busy.'

Chris put the box down carefully on the floor and spread his hands at the empty shop.

'Do I look busy?'

'No, but . . . '

'Shall I carry sleeping beauty, or will you?'

Emma contemplated him standing there, his hair slightly messy, his shirt unironed, his eyes fiercely blue and his teeth startlingly white. From out the back somewhere she could hear some classical piano music playing. She thought it might be Chopin.

She opened her mouth to say it was out of the question.

'Where would we put her? She's only

four, but she does take up quite a bit of room.'

'I've got a giltwood chaise-longue out the back. Edwardian, I believe. My old dad used to have an afternoon kip on it from time to time. I prefer to use it for seduction purposes myself. No, only joking. I've got a blanket, too, although not Edwardian, of course.'

Emma laughed, she couldn't help it. It made such a change for her to be chatting to an attractive man of her own age group. And she liked him, she really liked him.

'Oh, all right, then, but don't say I didn't warn you if she wakes up and screams the place down.'

Outside, the rain had eased off to a sulky drizzle, so Chris held a protective umbrella over Poppy as Emma manoeuvred her out of the car.

'She's like you, isn't she?' he whispered after gently tucking a rug around Poppy who was now lying in state on the to-be-reupholstered-one-day chaise-longue.

'So everyone tells me,' Emma said: 'Can't see it myself.'

She straightened up with a sigh to find Chris standing very close to her. Uncomfortably close, in fact. He was so near that she could see a pulse working in his throat where his shirt was unbuttoned at the neck. She looked up, away from a triangle of flesh that was on view. The laughter she was used to seeing in his eyes had faded a little and been replaced with a sudden seriousness.

Afterwards, she was never quite sure who had done the moving first, but she had a sneaking suspicion it might have been her. One moment she was looking at him and thinking that, oh, yes, now she came to think of it, he was rather attractive in an obvious way and the next moment, his lips gravitated towards hers and she was locked in a firm embrace that she felt no immediate desire to free herself from.

Just how had that happened?

As suddenly as the embrace began, it ended.

'Sorry,' Chris said. 'I just, sort of . . . couldn't help myself . . . '

Feeling slightly dazed Emma took a step back.

'My fault,' she said. 'My fault entirely . . . ' She bent down and tucked the rug over Poppy's arm. 'Bad idea to come in — I knew it was,' she said eventually, lifting her eyes from her sleeping daughter and back to Chris who was looking as terrified and embarrassed as she felt. 'Look, can we just forget that happened?'

Chris gave a relieved smile.

'Absolutely . . . If that's what you want. It was only a kiss, after all.' He forked his fingers through his hair and turned away.

'Right,' he said, filling the kettle for coffee. 'I'm afraid I can only offer instant coffee.'

Emma watched as he reached for a couple of mugs and put a teaspoon of instant in each. Then she quickly looked away just in case he managed to catch her staring.

Slowly her heartbeat was returning to its normal pace. She looked around at her surroundings.

They were in the cramped back room. The main reason it was cramped was because it acted as a mini kitchen, computer room and workshop, and also contained an old table and two chairs, not to mention the chaise-longue. Over the table there was a window in the wall, so that all Chris had to do was glance up from his computer which was placed at right angles, and through the window in order to survey the shop. An ideal set up, really, Emma thought.

'Now, then,' Chris said, all business now. 'Let's have a proper look at what you've brought.'

Rapidly he collected up the papers that were littering the old table his father had used for framing purposes, then carefully took the three pictures out and lay them in a row on its battered surface. Slowly, he scrutinised them. 'Don't be disappointed, I don't think any of them are by Cotman.'

'Oh,' Emma said.

'If they were, they'd be worth a lot.'

'Well, if they're not Cotmans, I'd rather not know how much, thanks! Sort of rubs salt in the wound.'

'It doesn't necessarily mean they're valueless, though.' Chris turned them over and inspected them closely. 'They're certainly old. And wherever they've been kept, they've come to no harm. This one — ' He pointed to the one of the boats on the water that had hung in the hall. ' — This one has been the most exposed, but it's been out of direct sunlight which is good. I would say, too, that it's by the same artist who painted the one of the church. They're both competent pieces of work, after the style of Cotman, but nothing out of the ordinary.'

'Oh,' Emma said again. 'Oh, well, it was only an idea.'

'I find this other one the most interesting though.'

'Why's that?'

'I don't know . . . None of them are

signed. But this is by a different artist and it's higher quality. Well, I can't say that for sure, of course . . . There was a school of artists about eighteen-twenty, if my memory serves me right, called the 'Norwich School', and I know that Cotman himself used to give lessons in order to supplement his income.'

'Sad, isn't it?' Emma said, thinking of Monica. 'That artists are never really recognised in their lifetime?'

'I'm just wondering if Cotman had any influence over this particular artist,' Chris said, still staring at the painting. 'There's a famous one by Cotman of 'Wherries on the Yare' which, before it's genius was recognised, sold in Norwich for under one pound about ten years before Cotman died. Can you believe that? Today it must be worth thousands upon thousands.' He switched his eyes quickly away from the painting to glance at Emma, then seemed to have some trouble switching them away again.

Eventually he wrenched his eyes back to the painting.

'This one puts me in mind of it. But don't get your hopes up. I'm no expert, it'll probably turn out to be worth next to nothing, but I'd be happy to get you a second opinion, of course.'

Emma wasn't quite sure if she felt weak from disappointment or from the kiss and the intensity of Chris's fiery gaze. She shrugged in what she hoped was a casual manner.

'Well, if it wouldn't be too much trouble . . . '

'I've already said, haven't I? It's no trouble, I'd be interested to know myself. Now, let's get that coffee.'

His fingers brushed hers as he handed her the mug, and a tingling sensation that travelled right through her arm to the pit of her stomach almost caused her to spill it all over the pictures.

Pull yourself together this instant, she told herself as she sat down shakily on the nearest chair. It was only a kiss, that was what he'd said.

'Nice biscuits,' Emma said a couple of minutes later, when she'd forced two bites down and was able to trust her voice not to come out as an over-excited squeak.

'It's very fortunate that I actually have biscuits,' Chris said. 'I don't usually keep them.'

'Are you a slave to a healthy diet, then?' Emma asked, regarding the crunchy, nutty shortbread-type biscuit that was probably loaded with calories, now she came to think of it.

'I was — but am no longer,' Chris said. 'I'm very glad to say,' he added.

'Change of lifestyle?'

'You could say that. I used to have a girlfriend who was a body beautiful fanatic.'

'Oh.' She'd just known it was too good to be true that someone as dishy as Chris could be completely without attachments.

'But not any more,' he went on as though to underline the point.

'Were you upset when it finished?' *Now why on earth did you have to ask that, Emma?*

Chris considered his half-eaten biscuit.

'Well, yes, I suppose I was,' he said sounding slightly surprised. 'But on reflection, we weren't really suited. I'm a bit too much of a tramp for her, and she was way, way too well-groomed for me.'

'Oh, I don't know,' Emma said nonchalantly — as though she'd only just thought of it. 'You look okay to me. She must have been a perfectionist.'

'She was . . . She wanted me to have my teeth straightened.'

'No! But you've got beautiful teeth,' Emma said before she could help herself. 'Really clean and spar . . . um-white.'

'Yep. That would be the whitening. She did persuade me into that one. The results are a bit more startling than I anticipated. I guess I'll have to take up chewing baccy in an attempt to pass for normal again. Only joking! I'm banking on red wine doing the job in half the time. Speaking of which . . . '

Poppy stirred in her sleep and flung out an arm. 'She'll wake up in a minute,' Emma said. 'Don't mention the pictures in the loft will you? I haven't told anyone about them. She knows about the one in the hall. It was Gavin who said it was worth getting it valued — he's convinced it's a Cotman because his mother thought it was.'

'The times I've heard that one. Does Gavin want his cut then? From the picture, I mean?'

Emma smiled.

'No, far from it. He wants to pay for everything. He'd pay for a new roof without batting an eyelid.'

'Why don't you let him then — lots of women would.'

'I'm not 'lots of women',' Emma said. 'Gavin pays very generously for Poppy's upkeep. His mother left the house to me and Poppy. The least I can do is to pay for its maintenance and my own keep.'

Chris took a last swig of his coffee.

'I understand,' he said. 'Good for

you. It's a two-edged sword, though, isn't it? Having property left to you — I mean. My father left me this shop. It hardly pays for itself, but he loved it, so I feel duty bound to keep it going. But it infringes on my life all the time.'

'Can't you get someone in to run it?'

'Probably. I have to do the sums first though.'

'I see.'

Chris went on to tell her about his other projects, and the fact that apart from his interest in antiques, television work, his history lectures and photographic journalism he was also a trained history teacher.

'The idea originally,' he said, 'was to be a writer in my spare time and teach full-time, but filming and writing television documentaries somehow became my main source of income and I do still enjoy it so much. I suppose I'm a sort of Jack of all trades. I try to work from here while I can and keep the shop open at the same time.' He paused for another bite of biscuit. 'I have a flat in London, but I'm thinking of letting it out, I'm down there so little . . . And I must confess my heart is here, along this coast-line. It's just so beautiful — especially in the early morning, when the tide's just creeping in.'

'I love it here, too,' Emma confessed. 'It suits us. My mum living only five minutes away, Poppy's school, which she'll start in September, just five minutes in the other direction. It's ideal and it's so peaceful.'

'Yes, there's a lot to be said for peace and quiet; ideal for writing bodice rippers I'd have thought.'

'In theory,' Emma agreed, remembering that *French Revolution* was now on hold. On impulse she told him about it. 'The upshot is,' she finished. 'I won't get paid until they accept it and they won't accept it for another eighteen months so I've got to get a wiggle on with the smuggler bodice ripper — as you so aptly call them.'

'What's a bodith ripper?' Poppy asked, sitting up and rubbing her eyes.

'Hi, poppet — you're awake,' Emma said in a falsely jolly voice in case Poppy had decided to wake up in a cranky mood.

Miraculously, however, Poppy had decided that her surroundings were far too interesting to be cranky about. After a glass of orange, which Chris went upstairs for and a biscuit of which he had a ready supply in a tin next to his computer, she walked round the shop with him, asking questions about all the 'very weird' things in his shop.

'That's really weird, isn't it, Mummy?' she said about a set of brass post-office scales. 'And look at these very weird thithors they've got a funny box thing on them.'

'They're special scissors for trimming candle wicks,' Chris explained. 'I'll show you if you like.'

By the time Chris had fetched a candle and shown Poppy how to cut the wick using the special scissors so that the spent wick dropped into the box, she was entranced by him, and displayed none of the shyness she usually showed with strangers.

'Come on, Poppy, we've taken up enough of Chris's time,' Emma said.

'Not at all,' Chris said. 'I'll give you a call when I know any more about the pictures.'

★   ★   ★

Chris watched as Emma helped Poppy into her carseat and then slid into the front seat and drove off. He was vaguely aware that he was sporting a slightly stupid expression on his face because he had just spent an entirely pleasurable couple of hours talking to an attractive, intelligent, funny lady. And what was more, miracle of miracles, the lady in question had seemed to consider him to be attractive, intelligent and funny, too.

And then there was the kiss.

How stupid was that when he'd already decided that becoming involved with Emma was the last thing he

118

wanted? But there'd been something about that kiss. It had been unpremeditated, warm, soft and, oh, so promising. But puzzling, too, because he wasn't entirely sure who it had been initiated by.

It was a question of the leaning. And now he came to think of it, surely she had been the one to lean first — almost imperceptibly — but definitely first. And he'd been the one to pull back first, and that had taken some doing, too. Maybe it was the awareness of the sleeping Poppy only an arm's length away that had made him stop and think again. *Or maybe, Chris, it was because you were so scared witless by what you were feeling for this woman you hardly know.*

Emma was scared, too. He'd seen it in her eyes before she blinked once or twice, as though she'd dreamt the moment.

But right now, he should stop dreaming and get back to work. He walked back through the shop repositioning the weird scales and even more weird scissors, somewhere accessible, just in case Poppy made another visit.

The shop bell jangled. His third customer of the day, Chris looked up and through the window to the shop in surprise.

'Oh, hello, Monica,' he called, smartly executing an about turn from his little back room; the last thing he wanted her to see were the three pictures where they still lay on the table.

Smilingly, he came towards the front of the shop. Monica was wearing an orange raincoat, carrying a purple umbrella and looking a trifle damp and windswept.

'You've braved the elements! My word, I'm flattered. What is it that I can do for you?'

Monica smiled. 'I was wondering,' she said. 'What you really thought of that little painting you saw at my daughter's place?'

Chris stroked his nose, trying to determine how on earth he would handle this one . . .

'Well,' he said tentatively. 'Funny you should ask that . . . '

Monica looked at him keenly.

'You don't need to tell her I asked.'

'Okay. If you don't want me to, I won't . . . But I'm sorry to have to say I don't think it's a Cotman.'

Monica gave a sigh.

'No, I didn't think so, either. D'you think it's worth anything at all?'

'I would say a few hundred — top whack. But I'm no expert.'

'No, but I trust you . . . Emma's been through a hard time. She's pretty tough, but not as tough as she makes out, and it's difficult for a single mother — I should know.'

'I'm sure,' Chris agreed, wondering whether it was his imagination or if there was a lot of reading between the lines he should be doing here.

'Of course, I'm hoping that she and Gavin will get back together again . . . it's perfectly possible. He's been seeing more of Poppy lately and he's indicated to me that . . . Well, he hasn't actually *said* anything . . . '

'Monica? Are you warning me off?'

Monica had the grace to blush.

'No, not exactly. Emma could do with all the friends she can get. I just wanted you to be aware of the situation. She's quite vulnerable, you know, and if there's a chance for her and Gavin to work things out well, I'd hate to see it go wrong for the sake of a mild flirtation.' Monica walked away from him and bent to examine a figurine that Chris knew held absolutely no interest for her. She placed the figurine firmly back in its place. 'I always regretted not giving Emma's father a second chance.'

'Woah, there!' Chris said. 'Emma's a big girl, she's divorced, and, yes, I like her, but we hardly know each other.'

'I'm not a fool, Chris, I could tell the moment I walked into the kitchen that you were very attracted to each other . . . By the way, whatever happened to the lovely blonde goddess who used to live here with you?'

'Oh, her,' Chris said carelessly. 'Oh, I chopped her up and put her in a meat pie.'

A grin spread across Monica's face.

'I suppose I deserved that . . . But, look, Gavin's grown up a bit, Emma was the one who wanted the marriage finished, he always thought the divorce was a mistake . . . '

'But divorce is pretty final, isn't it?' Chris put in.

Monica fiddled with her umbrella.

'I know, but I think he's serious this time . . . He realises the value of the family life he's missing.'

What about Emma? Chris wanted to ask. What about Emma's thoughts on the matter?

'Poppy adores him, you know . . . ' Monica went on relentlessly. 'I like you, Chris, I always have, you know that, but, well . . . they're my two gorgeous girls . . . I don't want you breaking Emma's heart . . . Think on it,' she added, turning to go.

Chris watched as Monica, in her

bright orange raincoat and with her purple umbrella in her paint-stained hand, made her way to the door.

'What about my heart?' he asked softly.

She opened the door and looked back cheekily over her shoulder.

'Oh, you? You're a man . . . Men only *think* they have hearts.'

8

Higher, Chris, higher,' Poppy shouted
with obvious glee. 'You're going higher
than I can push you,' Chris said. 'You're
wearing my arms out.'

Poppy giggled.

'No I'm not. You like pushing me,
really.'

And the funny thing was, Chris
thought, he did. He was enjoying
pushing Poppy on the swing in the park
and he was enjoying even more the
sensation of Emma, looking on indul-
gently and attempting, with the aid of
Chris's expensive camera, to take some
photos of her daughter flying through
the air.

Another two children were playing on
the swings, the mother standing near by
watching them with a bored expression
on her face. On a whim, Chris smiled at
her.

The mother suddenly became animated.

'Would you like me to take a photo of you all together?' she said.

'What a good idea,' Chris said quickly, before Emma could open her mouth to tell her that actually they weren't a family and it would not be necessary, thank you very much.

So the picture was taken, of Poppy on the swing, Emma standing holding the ropes immediately behind her and Chris standing tallest of all behind Emma.

The top of Emma's hair was tickling his chin, the perfume of her was in his nostrils and he could feel the curve of her bottom pressing against him. Although he would like to have a hand on her waist and his cheek next to hers, he could wait. It was a long time since he'd felt so at peace with the world and so . . . happy.

He had waited four days before contacting Emma again.

He knew it was exactly four days

because he felt as though he'd counted every hour and every minute of every one of them. Finally, before he got to the point of watching the second hand of his watch, he lifted the phone.

'As I was saying,' Chris said when Emma spoke. 'About the red wine . . . '

'Sorry?'

'Just before Poppy woke up the other day . . . ' He took a deep breath. 'I was trying to decide how to ask you to come out for the day — for a pub lunch or something?'

'And exactly what was it that you eventually decided to do in this case?'

'I decided to phone you. What *you* decide is more the question.'

There was a long silence during which Chris counted very slowly to ten.

'Where were you thinking of going?'

Yes! Chris thought. *Hallelujah!* It wasn't too outlandish a proposition. In principle, she'd agreed.

'I thought, now the weather's improved, maybe Maldon? It's not too far away, Poppy could go on the swings — plenty of room for her to run around in, and the town's nice . . . What d'you think?'

'Actually, it would be great. Poppy was meant to go out with Gavin this afternoon, but he rang to say there was a bit of a problem and he wouldn't be able to make it after all. He's going to ring me later, make a plan for tomorrow, maybe.'

'Oh.' Chris fought down the feeling that he was only second best. Of course he *was* only second best — certainly with Poppy. Bound to be — stood to reason. But for Emma? Well, Chris knew already, he didn't want to be second best with Emma.

'I was just trying to think what we could do today so Poppy wouldn't be too disappointed,' Emma went on. 'So, yes, we'd love to come to Maldon for lunch.'

Hardly believing his luck, Chris had turned the sign on the shop door to *Closed* put his camera round his neck and a couple of extra lenses into the boot. He told himself that this was a 'working' day off, because he knew he'd find some great shots around the area.

He explained as much to Emma when he picked them up.

'I've been meaning to take some shots of Maldon for a while. There's some Thames barges in dock, they always make good calendar fodder.'

'Fine,' Emma said, transferring Poppy's child seat to Chris's Volvo. 'I hope we won't disturb your concentration.'

So they'd had a companionable drive to Maldon, with Poppy in the back seat crooning quietly to Lucy lamb and occasionally kicking the back of Chris's seat, but he didn't mind that. Oh, no, so long as Emma was sitting beside him with her freshly-washed hair and smelling of whatever the light flowery perfume he'd come to associate with her, he felt himself to be in seventh heaven.

They'd had a walk along the banks of the Blackwater, with Poppy skipping excitedly in front of them, then they'd stopped for some lunch at a waterside pub.

Chris told her a few more smuggling tales and enquired politely as to the progress of the bodice ripper.

'What is a bodith ripper Chrith?' Poppy asked completely innocently.

Emma looked at him as if to say 'Okay, Chris — get out of that one.'

'Um, something to do with Velcro, perhaps, or maybe patchwork quilting,' Chris said without missing a beat.

Emma snorted into her drink and luckily at that moment the fish and chips had arrived. Chris made up a story about a fat chip who wanted to be thin, and a thin chip who wanted to be fat and a green gerkin called Wally, who actually wanted to be a pickled onion.

'Why, why?' Poppy asked. 'Why did he want to be a pickled onion?'

'Because pickled onions are so strong, they can even make a grown man cry.'

'Oh,' Poppy said, her eyes full of wonder. 'Will you cry if you eat one?'

'We'll have to see,' Chris said, taking a bite, pulling a series of grotesque faces, then proceeding to cry into his handkerchief.

'You're just pretending,' Poppy said delightedly. 'You're just being silly like my nanny.'

'Glad to be in such good company,' Chris said with a distinctly meaningful look at Emma.

After the swings, it was a long walk back to the car and the sun, which had been growing in strength as the day wore on, was burning hot now on their bare arms and legs.

'I'd best take you home now,' Chris said, although it was the last thing he really wanted to do.

'Yes,' Emma said. 'I've had two messages on my phone from Gavin, but I haven't looked at them yet . . . It won't hurt him to have to wait for a bit.'

Chris fought down the urge to shout 'Yippee', and just smiled in a way he hoped was enigmatic.

'We've really enjoyed today,' Emma went on. 'Thanks for inviting us and being so good with Poppy.'

Chris cleared his throat.

'We must do it again,' he said. *Woah! Easy now Chris. Don't come on too strong.* 'I've enjoyed it, too . . . Oh, I've got your boat picture, the one that was hanging in the hall. I'm afraid I was right, that one and the one of the church are nice little pictures but you'd be lucky to get more than a hundred on either of them. Incidentally, if you do want to sell them I can probably arrange it for you — make sure you get a price that's halfway decent.'

Emma pulled a face.

'Maybe the ones from the loft, but not the one Gavin is so certain is a Cotman,' she said. 'That wouldn't seem fair, really. It was his mum's and probably holds sentimental value for him.'

'Well, anyway, they're in the boot of my car. The other one of the boats that you found in the loft, we're still looking at — but it's almost certainly not by John Cotman, either.'

'Well, I'm not surprised really.' Emma sighed. 'But you're right, I'd better replace the one from the hall before Gavin misses it and puts me through a cross examination, then tells me what a hopeless mother I am, not to allow him to get my roof fixed.' She looked round to make sure Poppy wasn't listening. 'If he were to do that, I'd probably wind up telling him what a bad father he is not to turn up when he says he will, and the last thing I want is a slanging match in front of Poppy. Unfortunately, she's already witnessed a couple of those.'

Once again Chris said nothing.

* * *

When they got back to where they'd parked the car, Poppy was obviously drooping. Reluctantly, Emma judged it best to agree with Chris and end the outing now, while they were all enjoying themselves. Besides, she really didn't want Chris to witness Poppy change from a bundle of beguiling fun into a wailing unreasonable tyrant at the drop of a hat, which she was only too capable of doing.

They were all very quiet on the journey home, Emma thought. Surprisingly Poppy didn't fall asleep, but kept singing *The Wheels On The Bus* with such tenacity that, under normal circumstances, Emma would have been silently screaming for her to finish, but today she found it quite endearing.

'Oh, Lord!' They'd reached the cottage and Emma spotted Gavin's car straight away. 'Gavin's turned up after all,' she said. 'He must have used his key to get in.'

Chris pulled up and went to the boot while Emma helped Poppy out of the car.

'Here's your hall picture; I'll give you the other one you found in the loft later . . . Best I don't come in,' he added.

134

Emma tucked the picture under her arm and smiled at him in relief.

'Yes, it could be awkward,' she agreed. 'But thanks for a lovely day. I'll phone you.'

★ ★ ★

The door to the cottage opened almost before Chris's car had disappeared from sight.

'Hi.' Emma hoped the air of slight triumph she was feeling, that this time he'd been the one to do the waiting for a change, didn't show on her face.

Gavin looked annoyed. 'Didn't you get my message?'

'No,' Emma lied. 'My phone was at the bottom of my bag. It's probably still on there. Anyway, we thought you weren't coming.'

'We've been to Maldon with Chrith,' Poppy chirped in. 'And Chrith pushed me really high on the swing. Really, really high. It was weird.'

'Hello, Poppy,' Gavin said, belatedly

ruffling Poppy's hair. 'Who's Chrith? I mean Chris.'

A small smile played at the corners of Emma's lips and she made no attempt to control it.

'A friend,' she said. 'Your friend, actually . . . Chris Hemmings, the guy you email from time to time. I went to his talk on the coastline . . . The one you recommended, remember?'

'Oh,' Gavin said, looking even more thunderous. He glanced pointedly at his watch. 'I suppose it's too late to take Poppy out now?'

'Well, she is rather tired.'

'I've been waiting for two hours!'

'I'm sorry,' Emma lied again. 'Waiting can be so tedious, can't it?'

Gavin looked at her sharply.

'Come in and have some tea, though, if you like,' Emma said, relenting a little. She pushed past him into the cool interior of the narrow hall.

'What's that under your arm?'

'What? Oh, that,' Emma said nonchalantly. 'That's the non-Cotman'. Perhaps you'd put it back for me while I put the kettle on.'

'I suppose you got it looked at in Maldon? But I shouldn't believe what any local antique dealers tell you.'

'No,' Emma said. 'No way! That's why Chris got a second opinion for me from a guy in Norwich.'

'Chris? What does he know all of a sudden? You seem to be taking a lot of notice of his expertise.'

'Well, he is an antiques dealer,' Emma said mildly. 'A knowledgeable one as it happens. My mother thinks the world of him.'

'Oh does she?'

'Yes, she does, actually . . . Oh, come on, Gavin. Stop being so grumpy. Have a cup of tea.'

Gavin gave a grin.

'All right. It threw me a bit when you weren't here, that's all.'

Emma bit down the retort that since they were now divorced, it was no longer any business of his what she did with her time, and busied herself with tea and the scones she'd been hoping to share with Chris.

'What have you been doing with yourself, poppet?' Gavin asked. Poppy looked at him over the top of her mug of juice. 'Mummy threw cold water all over me,' she said. 'And I got really, really wet.'

'Ah,' Gavin said, glancing at Emma. 'I expect Mummy was just playing.'

'No, she wasn't — she fell down the stepth and squashed me!'

Thank you Poppy!

'It wasn't that bad,' Emma said quickly. 'I was in the roof emptying the water from the leak and I slipped on the way down — that's all.'

'I thought you were going to get that fixed?' Gavin said.

'I am, I am. I'm just waiting for the roof guy to fit me in when he can, that's all . . . Look, I'm sure it'll be done by the winter months, I promise.'

'I've told you to bill it to me. Suppose you'd injured yourself? I don't mind paying — I told you.'

'It's not the money — the roofer is very busy and can't fit us in just yet!'

Gavin sighed. 'You are so stubborn.'

Emma grinned. 'So I've been told, by . . . now who was it? Oh, you, actually.'

'I suppose that's why you're suddenly getting the Cotman valued?'

'It's not a Cotman.'

'Mum always thought it was.'

'What's a Cotman?' Poppy asked.

'I'll take it to London and get it valued myself,' Gavin said. 'That's, if you don't mind, of course. I know it's not mine and I have no claim to it.'

Emma smiled. 'Gavin, the one thing I've never accused you of is being mean. I know you have the best of intentions. If you want to take it to London, please do so. If it proves to be a Cotman, that would be great — but please don't bank on it, I think Chris knows what he's about.'

'Hm,' Gavin said, taking the picture from the wall and standing it in front of the door so he wouldn't forget it.

No more was said about the picture. Gavin played a game of snap and spot the difference with Poppy in the sitting room, while Emma ploughed her way through a pile of ironing in the kitchen. Nonetheless she was relieved when Gavin got up to go.

'Watch yourself with this Chris character,' he said as he was leaving. 'You don't really know that much about him.'

Emma looked at him levelly.

'Don't I?'

'Well, do you?'

'This is a ridiculous conversation, Gavin. I don't cross-examine you about any photos you happen to be carrying in your wallet, do I?'

Gavin flushed. 'You had no business going through my wallet.'

'I didn't 'go through' it. It fell open on the floor! Not as young as your usual type, I wouldn't have said, and maybe a tad serious. Still, I don't suppose it'll last long will it? They never do. As for Chris, well, I'm not carrying his picture around with me, that I can assure you. He's a good friend — I like him. But he's not interested in me. Why should he be?'

'Well, if he's not interested in you, maybe he's interested in the Cotman. I'll definitely get another opinion on it.'

Trying not to lose her temper, Emma shrugged.

'Yes, you do that, Gavin. If it makes you happy, you do that.'

'Mummy, why are you cross?' Poppy said, watching at the front door as Gavin put the painting on the back seat of his car then got in and slammed his own door shut.

'I'm not cross, poppet, I'm just thinking,' Emma replied, plastering a smile on her face and waving in a friendly manner as her ex-husband's car swung onto the road.

9

'Do I look all right?' It was two weeks later. Monica glanced across as Emma appeared in the doorway wearing a black and white flowery print dress, which showed off her long legs and gently tanned shoulders.

'Yes, you do, you gorgeous girl'

'I thought *I* was your gorgeous girl, Nanny!' Poppy said.

'You both are,' Monica said diplomatically. 'You look divine,' she said again to Emma. 'Who would have thought I'd have such a divine daughter.'

'Divine,' Emma said, openly aghast. 'Hardly! Anyway, I don't want to look divine. He'll think I've made a special effort.'

'Well, you have.'

'But I don't want to look over the top.'

'You don't look over the top. You have a sort of glow about you, that's all. And it's nice to see you in sandals with a heel and a dress instead of jeans and an ancient t-shirt.'

'Well, we're going to a restaurant, not a pub, so I thought I should take a bit more care. Anyway, what's brought about your sudden change of heart regarding Chris?'

'This photograph, I think,' Monica said, looking at the photo of her daughter, granddaughter and Chris that was propped up on the dresser. 'You look so happy, and you need a bit of fun.'

'You look really pretty, Mummy,' Poppy said.

'Thank you, poppet . . . My dress isn't too short, is it?'

Monica sighed. 'No! Anyway, it's too late — he's here. Now, have a good time. I'll admit I wasn't too sure about this turn of events with you and Chris, but an evening out will do you the world of good — so long as you don't take it too seriously.'

'Oh, Lord,' Emma said, hardly listening and pulling at her dress. 'I'm not cut out for all this dressing up and stuff. I feel all wrong.'

'Mummy feels all wrong,' Poppy said conversationally as Emma opened the door to Chris's ring.

'Wow, she looks pretty well all right to me,' Chris said. Emma noticed he had taken extra pains himself, in that he was wearing a crease-free blue and grey striped shirt that she'd never seen him in before.

His hair was freshly-washed, too, Emma noticed, and she detected a faint waft of nutmeg about his person. Goodness it must be after-shave; this was all becoming rather grown-up and serious.

'Well, I'm ready,' she said. 'I won't be late, Mum. Help yourself to wine.'

'A glass or three,' said Monica, who was already halfway through her first. 'I might even finish the bottle as I'm staying here the night.'

Oh, dear, that was Monica's way of saying it didn't matter what time they got back or even if they got back at all. Thinking of the 'kiss' which, although it had not been repeated, had hardly left her thoughts, Emma's face became even hotter.

Chris opened the car door for her and, feeling rather like minor royalty, Emma got in. She sat stiffly in her seat, wondering what on earth to talk about. She'd thought it would be so nice for Chris and her to have an evening on their own, but already she was beginning to miss the constant chaperonage of her small daughter. Funny how relaxed she could be in Chris's company when there was a child as a distraction, whereas now, without Poppy, she felt as though he was a complete stranger — what with his ironed shirt and all.

Chris gave a sudden chuckle.

'Weird isn't it? As Poppy would say.'

'Sorry?'

'I was really looking forward to

having you to myself, but now I have, I find I'm missing Poppy.'

'Well, I'm not,' Emma said resolutely. 'It's lovely to go out for a change and to a real, grown-up restaurant. Nothing weird about it. It's a treat.'

Chris smiled. 'Good . . . Can I ask you something?'

'Of course,' Emma said cautiously.

'How long is it since you split from Gavin?'

Emma shifted in her seat. Even now she didn't really like talking about the break up of her marriage.

'Well, it's difficult to say. Things started going wrong just after Poppy was born, I suppose. Gavin was working away a lot and there were always temptations and opportunities for him.' She swallowed, even though it no longer hurt as it had done. 'The first two times, I forgave him, but when it happened a third time, I just couldn't stand all the lies and deceit, so . . . '

'So?'

'I kicked him out. Well, I moved

down here with my mum for a while. Then, of course, Gavin's mum became ill, so I helped Mum look after her where I could. When she died, she left the cottage to me and Poppy, so that we could enjoy an independence of a sort, I think. It seemed sensible to go for divorce. Cleaner, somehow. I knew I'd never take him back. The rest you know . . . What about you?'

Chris's fingers tightened on the steering wheel.

'Timing's never been right. Right girl, wrong place. Right time, wrong girl. That kind of stuff. I thought I was ready the last time — thought she was, too. But, no, we were attracted to each other, but that's not enough, is it? . . . It takes more than that . . . I thought I could compromise, that I could live with her constant pursuit of perfection . . . ' He gave a deprecating laugh. 'I nearly convinced myself I could. But in the end it was Fiona who couldn't stand the fact that I just didn't care about achieving a target body weight, or finding the exact right shade of grey for the bathroom wall.

'She hated that I was happy pottering around in my dad's old flat, living here in Little Lexden, going out on early morning rambles along the coast and not really having too much of a plan. She kept saying things like 'Where do you see us in five years' time?' and 'Your lifestyle should really be more healthily-balanced, Chris.'. In retrospect it was a relief when she left.'

'Well, perhaps you weren't ready, not really, to settle down, as they say.'

'Oh, I was ready,' Chris said firmly. 'It was just the wrong girl, I know that now.'

There was something in his tone which made Emma think of the 'kiss' again. She wondered if it would ever be repeated and, if so, would tonight be the time? A tingle went down her spine at the thought. *Get a grip, Emma. Control yourself!*

'We're nearly there,' Chris said a moment later. 'I'm hoping they've saved us the window overlooking the estuary so I can show you the magic of the water flowing in over the mud flats.'

Oh, well, perhaps action replay time hadn't yet arrived. Emma smiled to herself. She could wait . . .

★   ★   ★

Afterwards Emma couldn't remember what they'd had to eat. Only that it was fish and delicious, that the wine was crisp and light and that the evening had taken on a magical quality as they'd sat opposite one another, talking and softly laughing; occasionally falling silent, then both talking at once, breaking off — then laughing again.

It wasn't that she felt like a teenager again, exactly. It wasn't that she went out so little that any evening containing a hint of romance was bound to throw her off balance. It was more to do with the man sitting opposite her. It was to do with their conversation, with the way he could laugh at himself, make her laugh at herself, encourage her to take a step back, and look at her life and how richly rewarding it was and yet feel no guilt.

In the past, when Gavin had arrived home from a war torn country, it was as though he was constantly reprimanding her for not being continually grateful for her relatively problem free life. It was as though he sat in judgement and that his own transgressions should be allowed to go without comment, because there were so many more 'real' catastrophes going on in the world.

Little by little, as the evening wore on, Emma found herself relaxing and giving in to the enchantment of the moment. Chris made her feel interesting, amusing and romantic, yet rather sexy all at the same time. And she didn't want those feelings to stop.

It was a beautiful evening. The stars looked as though they'd been polished especially bright before being hung against the velvet sky, and the night air was soft, yet fresh from the water's edge. Listening to the gentle ripples of the incoming tide, they walked along the shoreline path, Chris's jacket slung across Emma's shoulders, his hand holding hers.

'What a wonderful evening,' Emma said, feeling warm from the wine and heady from the sensation of Chris's hand in hers.

'It's lovely to have someone to share it with.'

'My, aren't we polite?'

'It's because I'm scared.'

Emma almost stopped breathing.

'Scared? Why scared?'

Slowly, gently, he turned her towards him.

'Because . . . you take my breath away,' he said. 'Because . . . because . . . '

And then the stars were blotted out as his head moved closer and Emma gave a sigh of pure bliss before his lips met hers.

★   ★   ★

'Hi, there.'

'Oh, hello, Gavin, it's you.'

'Well, don't sound so disappointed. Who were you expecting?'

'Oh, I was expecting Mum to ring.' Really, this recent tendency of hers to lie was getting out of control, Emma thought. But how could she admit to Gavin of all people that, actually, she'd been hoping for a call from Chris? That she'd been on tenterhooks all morning, wondering if she should be the first to call, or whether she was reading way, way too much into the last few days. But surely, surely, she hadn't been.

The snatched kisses. The way they'd gazed at each other, the way they could hardly bear to let go of one another's hands. The lingering glances when they'd thought no one else was looking, the phone calls, the text messages, all innocent in themselves, just friendly reassurances that the other was well, that the other was still there. The flimsy excuses they made to meet up under the least pretext . . . The occasion when

Chris dropped round at the cottage unexpectedly saying: 'It's the car's fault. It has a will of its own. Can you and Poppy come out to play?'

The tenderness in his eyes when he watched Poppy dragging Lucy Lamb along behind her, by an ear ... The way Emma's heart hammered under her ribs at the touch of his lips on her cheek.

She stood holding the phone, listing reasons to believe the unbelievable, she smiled dreamily to herself. 'Emma? Did you hear what I said?'

'What? Oh, sorry. I'm a bit distracted this morning.' Well, at least that wasn't a lie.

'The picture, the Cotman. I've had it looked at.'

'Oh. Right.'

'It's not a Cotman.'

'I know, Chris already told me.'

'Did he also tell you that it might not be a Cotman, but it's still sure to be worth a lot of money?'

'No,' Emma said with a curiously sick

feeling starting to form in the pit of her stomach.

'What exactly did he say, then?'

Emma shifted her weight to her other leg.

'That it wasn't worth much.'

'He didn't give you a written valuation?'

'No. He offered to sell it for me if I needed the money; that's all.'

There was a long pause during which Emma tried not to remember that Chris had said that the pictures were only really worth a couple of hundred at best.

'Anyway, how much is a 'lot' of money?'

'How does ten thousand sound?'

Emma sat down rather suddenly on the hard wooden kitchen chair.

'How much?'

'You heard correctly . . . I take it Chris's valuation was somewhat less?'

'There must be some mistake,' Emma said firmly.

'Yes, it was his mistake thinking I

wouldn't get a second opinion . . . I told you not to trust him.'

Emma said nothing.

'You don't sound very happy about it being valuable.'

'I'm not, really,' Emma said, trying to pull herself together and ignore the pain under her ribs. 'I mean, what are we going to do with it?'

'Well, it's yours, Emma. It belongs to you. Sell it and pay for your roof.'

Emma gave a gasp of surprise that bordered on the tearful.

'I can't sell it. It's always been in the hall. I suppose I can't leave it there now. Besides, what would your mother say?'

There was a long unhappy silence between the two of them.

'I've got an idea,' Gavin said eventually in a more gentle voice. 'How about I keep the picture? I'd like to keep it; it'll be a reminder of Mum and of you and Poppy. My flat's secure — it'll be quite safe. I'll give you the ten thousand and you can do your roof.

How does that sound?'

Emma felt confused. Confused and angry and . . . upset . . .

'It's very kind of you, but . . . '

'But what? It's not kind, anyway. It's an investment. I can't go wrong. Paintings by well-known artists don't lose value. Not this one, anyway.'

'So who is the artist, then?' Emma asked, even though she didn't really care right now.

'Can't remember off hand. Why?'

'Well, I'd like to tell Chris . . . Come on, you must remember. Think!'

'Something beginning with a W, I think. Hang on, I'll have a look. I wrote it down somewhere . . . It looks like Webster . . . I don't know. Oh, you know what my writing's like. Anyway, will you let me send you a cheque and hang on to the picture?'

Emma stood up again and looked over at the jug of white daisies Chris had bought her. The jug was sitting on the windowsill and the flowers looked bright and pretty against the light, but on closer examination some of the petals were falling and their grainy centres were fading.

'All right then,' Emma said. 'Thank you, Gavin.'

★   ★   ★

Chris was perplexed. No, it was more than that; he was bewildered.

What could possibly have happened, he asked himself, for Emma to change from the delightful, carefree, almost flirtatious, companion of the last week into the watchful, anxious and, yes, even guarded, person she was now? What was wrong? Had he suddenly developed halitosis, or maybe had some kind of a personality transplant without noticing?

They were sitting in the garden of the cottage. It was early evening and the sun was low and golden in the sky. Poppy was mixing some strange combination of grass cuttings, mud, and lavender seeds together in an old yoghurt pot and Chris chewed at his bottom lip and watched as Emma poured the tea.

'What's the problem?' he asked.

'No problem,' Emma answered, not looking at him as she passed his tea.

'Come on, you can do better than that.' He caught one of her hands in his and held onto it by the fingers.

'Gavin took the picture to London.'

'I know, you told me, remember? And I said, 'Good, I wouldn't trust me either.' Well, the thing is — they've told him it's not a Cotman.'

Chris nodded. 'Go on . . . '

'But it is a Webster.'

'And who's Webster when he's at home?'

'Well, he's obviously collectable . . . Not to mention valuable.'

Chris felt his eyes narrowing. 'How valuable?'

Embarrassed, Emma looked away. 'It's only approximate — but around about ten thousand.'

Chris whistled. 'Wow,' he said slowly.

'I've heard of a Max Weber, he was Russian by birth and moved to America, but his stuff is modern — hardly Cotman's style, and it's highly unlikely it would turn up here . . . That would be just too bizarre . . . I've never heard of a Webster though . . . Ten thousand eh? . . . Gavin's got a customer then, has he?'

'No, he wants to keep it himself. In memory to his mother.'

'Oh, so all the time he thought it was just another old watercolour, he had no interest, but now he thinks it's worth a bit, he wants it in memory of his mother? Do me a favour.'

An angry flush spread across Emma's face. 'What right have you to judge Gavin? That's not how it is at all. He wants to buy the painting from me. He's willing to pay me the ten thousand straight away.'

Momentarily Chris was lost for words. Ten thousand — just like that! How could a small time antiques dealer, occasional geographical filmmaker and historical researcher, possibly compete with that?

'I suppose he must be stinking rich?'

'Not stinking rich.'

'Rich enough not to miss the odd ten thousand.'

'Well, I suppose that's not very rich in the scheme of things. It's only when you've got a leaking roof, an empty bank balance and a rejection slip that it sounds like a lot.'

'I'm sorry,' said Chris. 'I was being unfair. Just because I've never heard of Webster doesn't mean he doesn't exist. I'm surprised it's worth that much though, especially since it wasn't recognised as anything out of the ordinary in Norwich. My advice to you is to take the money and run.'

'I intend to,' Emma said. 'Take the money, I mean. I wasn't thinking of running anywhere.'

'Good,' Chris said, thinking at the same time that it wasn't good, that Emma was looking at him now with, if not suspicion exactly, then with a little more wariness in her eyes.

Should he say what he'd been meaning to tell her this afternoon? Suddenly it didn't seem the moment.

A little later he made his excuses — a deadline for a feature article on UFO's sighted in the East Anglian skies — and left muttering a curse on all ex-husbands, Emma's in particular.

10

It was a conundrum, that was what it was. Chris strode along the sea wall at Goldhanger. The salty air from the river Blackwater stirred his too long hair and stung his eyes. Despite the rash of modern buildings in the old country fishing and farming village, its heart with the medieval inn at its centre still remained attractive enough to take some shots of and, on a professional level, Chris felt he'd had a good morning.

But where was his life going on a more personal level, he wondered?

It wasn't that he shirked involvement, or that he lacked commitment. It was just that when a woman entered the equation, life seemed to get so messy so very quickly. What should he do? Whatever he did he'd be wrong, he knew that. So best to do what he was best at — nothing. But then, what would be the consequence of that?

He missed Emma and Poppy quite dreadfully. He'd been surprised and flattered by the way Poppy had taken to him, and amazed by his own affection for her. Emma had done a good job in bringing up her daughter, and that Poppy would always come first with her he didn't doubt. But still, he missed them and he didn't want Emma to go through the rest of her life thinking he was some kind of confidence trickster — that was really too awful to contemplate.

So, why was he faffing about? It wasn't a hard decision at all actually. He had to tell her. But how to tell her, that was the problem. He'd seen her reaction when he'd dared to question the reasons behind Gavin suddenly wanting to keep the painting. He didn't want to be on the receiving end of that sudden rapier like fury again, thank you very much.

And then, what about Gavin?

Why was Gavin suddenly so interested in Emma's life?

Chris glanced at his watch, took a sharp intake of breath and turned back towards his car. He couldn't afford to mooch around here all day. He had places to go, people to see and a slowly failing antique shop to open. Life was just a bowl of chocolates, or a box of cherries, or whatever the lying song said.

* * *

'Mummy's next book's about thewing.'

'Sewing?' queried Monica. 'Are you quite sure, gorgeous girl?'

Poppy nodded. 'You rip the bodices up into squares. A bodice is the top of a dress, like a little T-shirt. Then you thew them up in a pattern like a blanket. Only it's called a quilt — isn't it Mummy?'

'Yes,' Emma said distractedly.

Monica grinned. 'I like that definition. I must remember it.'

Poppy wandered off into the garden to inspect her seed patch for any new growth of weeds.

'Now spit it out,' Monica said, giving her daughter a meaningful glance. 'What's the problem?'

Emma sighed. 'The Cotman's not a Cotman. Gavin took it to London. But, wait for it — it's a Webster — worth ten thousand.'

Monica nearly dropped the glass she was drying. 'What?'

'I know,' Emma said miserably.

'But that's great. It'll cover the cost of the roof.'

'Yep, as it happens.'

'Mmm. Why the long face then?'

'The thing is, Mum. Chris has never heard of this Webster.'

'Neither have I, but there are lots of artists I've never heard of . . . Doesn't mean a thing. Art history is only an interest of mine. It's not a specialist subject for Chris either.'

Glumly, Emma took the glass Monica had polished almost to

oblivion and stretched up to the shelf that was too high for Monica. Having safely restored the glasses Chris had expressed a liking for, to their normal resting place, she gave another sigh. She thought she might not use them again for some time.

★   ★   ★

'Gavin Fielding.'

Start smilingly confident, thought Chris. Confidence travelled down the phone, everyone knew that. 'Good afternoon, Gavin. This is Chris Hemmings here.'

There was a pause just long enough for Chris to realise, that Gavin's mind had been so occupied on other things, the name had taken a few seconds to register.

'Oh, hi there.'

'I wondered if we might have a word about this 'Webster' you've had valued for Emma?'

'Ah.'

'If you're busy, it's no problem. Tell me when you won't be and I'll ring you then . . . I'm rarely that busy you see.'

'Actually you were lucky to catch me. I'm just slinging a few things into a case; I'll be leaving for the airport shortly. I have an assignment lined up for me in Dubai.'

Mr Mission Impossible, thought Chris. *How to compete with that?* 'Webster,' he continued doggedly. 'Not an artist I'm familiar with. Perhaps you could fill me in with some detail?'

There was another pause, longer this time.

'Yes, well . . . ' If ever there was a rueful smile in a voice, Chris could hear it now in Gavin's. 'OK, you've got me.'

'Have I?' asked Chris in neutral tones.

'Oh, you know what Emma's like. She's so damn stubborn . . . The cottage needs a new roof. She makes a mere pittance from her writing. She's just had a book rejected . . . How else was I to get the money to her?'

'I don't know, but lying seems more than a little extreme. Or was there more to it than that?'

'Sorry? I don't understand you.'

A tide of sudden fury overtook Chris. 'Oh I think you do. You knew I'd told Emma the truth, that the painting was not a Cotman but an average 'in the style of', worth about one fifty on a good day. What better way to discredit me in her eyes than be willing to pay ten thousand for a 'Webster' — and where that name came from I can't think!'

'Emma's very vulnerable.'

'Oh is she?'

'I care about her.'

'You mean you care about her so much you can't bear to see her having a good time, having some fun.'

'This conversation is deteriorating.'

'Believe me mate, if you were standing opposite me I'd be punching you on the nose about now!'

Now you've done it, Chris, he'll hang up on you, and you're no better off than when you started this stupid, pointless conversation.

A sigh flew down the line. 'The thing is, I was home for longer than usual this time and seeing more of Poppy and of Emma, I began to remember the good times, realise I was missing out . . . I'll admit it; I had thoughts of us getting back together again. Just now and then, of course.'

'You mean when . . . ' *No, don't say 'when you're bored' Chris. You'll just antagonise him.* 'When it seemed appropriate?' he amended through his gritted teeth.

'Yes, something like that.'

'Forgive my saying so,' said Chris silkily, 'but isn't that rather a 'dog in the manger' attitude?'

'Poppy is my daughter,' bristled Gavin. 'Emma is, I mean was my wife, after all.'

'Yes. Divorced now, aren't you? . . . And Emma never denies you access to Poppy does she? It doesn't strike you then, that you're being a tad selfish? A wee bit 'cake and eat it'?'

Silence. Then: 'I really don't have time for this,' said Gavin. 'I'm going to Dubai. I have a flight to catch.'

Chris resisted the impulse to say it couldn't be quick enough for him. 'Have you told Emma you're going?'

Gavin sounded surprised. 'No, not yet.'

'Well, perhaps when you do, you could also tell her about the 'Webster', and that you so love the picture that it's worth ten thousand to you anyway, so you've already transferred the money to her account. I've always found Emma to be very understanding. I'm sure you'll find the right words to talk her round.'

'You don't want me to tell her anything else?'

'What else is there to tell?'

'It didn't ruin your relationship with her then?'

'Of course not,' said Chris with a confidence he was far from feeling. 'Emma knows me well enough to trust me. Once you've explained you made up 'Webster' for the very best of reasons — because you can't bear to think of Poppy living in a cottage with a leaking roof — the mother instinct will kick in and she'll be fine.'

'I'll do that then.'

'When?'

'As soon as I can.'

'Like, before you go to the airport?'

He then heard an exasperated sigh down the phone. 'If you say so,' agreed Gavin.

'Oh yes,' said Chris with a grin. 'I do say so. Have a good trip and say hi to Dubai for me.'

Gavin didn't reply.

★   ★   ★

Emma combed her hair and applied some mascara. She hadn't heard from Chris for three days now and she knew it was up to her to do the contacting. The thing was she didn't know what to say.

171

Should she just say 'hi stranger, long time no see,' as though nothing had happened, or should she tell him about Gavin and the curious way he'd suddenly phoned her yesterday, admitting that he'd made up Webster as an artist simply in order to pay for the roof?

Dimly, Emma remembered being cross about that at the time and then, when she'd felt the sudden joy that it had been Gavin who'd been lying not Chris, she'd felt a rush of gladness of heart.

Now, she wondered why on earth she'd made so much fuss about Gavin paying for the roof in the first place. Who cared who paid for the roof as long as she knew that Chris hadn't lied to her?

But what on earth was Chris thinking now? Obviously he was cross because the phone calls had stopped, the silly text messages and the emails, and he hadn't come round either, or tooted his horn as he went past the cottage. She felt oddly bereft about that, then reasoned that he was probably feeling cross too. Goodness knows she'd given him reason when she'd snapped at him about the value of the picture. She remembered the veiled expression in his eyes when he'd left. At the time she'd put it down to guilt, if anything, but now she realised it was more likely to have been hurt. And that was the last thing she'd wanted to do to him.

It was obviously going to be up to her.

She didn't want to call him on the phone; he might have a customer in the shop. But there was nothing to stop her from calling in the shop and asking about the other two paintings. Yes, that was it. Ask about them and mention, in passing, about Gavin and his stupid ideas on how he would manage to persuade her to allow him to pay for the roof.

Right! Now, was an ideal opportunity. Monica had taken Poppy swimming and would give her some tea afterwards. Poppy had gone off with her delightedly discussing which colour nail varnish they would apply when they returned for tea.

Before she could think about it any more Emma quickly walked through the cottage, locked the back door and picked up her car keys.

His black Volvo was tucked round the side of the shop in front of the old outhouse. Emma parked her car alongside it.

The shop bell sounded really loudly as she stepped onto the mat and then on into the shady interior. Through the window at the rear end of the shop she could see Chris bent over his computer.

'Be with you in a minute,' he shouted without turning his head.

Dodging round sticking out pieces of furniture, Emma slowly made her way through the shop towards the back. She realised she was shaking slightly. She watched him as he examined the screen before him. He was editing photos, she realised, and the one on screen at the moment was the one taken at Maldon of Chris, Poppy and herself. As she watched, Chris homed in on a close up of her own laughing face and enlarged it until it took up the whole screen.

'Can't you find anything better than that to do with your time?'

With a start, Chris swivelled round to face her and his smile of spontaneous delight made her heart turn over. In an instant he was up and she was in his arms.

'Don't do that to me again,' said Chris.

'Do what?' she teased.

'Do that. Leave me alone for four days then creep up on me.'

'I didn't creep up on you,' Emma said with her nose pressed up against his crumpled blue shirt. 'And anyway it was only three days.'

Chris held her away from him for a moment. 'Ah, so you were counting the days too.'

'Yes,' she admitted, 'and it was horrible.'

'Come here,' said Chris leading her

to the chaise longue. 'I can't stand these long separations.'

* * *

'Gavin rang me,' Emma said a little later.

'Who Gavin? Who he?' Chris said, nibbling at her ear lobe.

'My stupid ex. He made up Webster you know.'

'Thought he might have done.'

'Well, goodness knows why, but he thought it was the only way he could pay for the roof.'

'Well, he was right wasn't he?' said Chris, who had now progressed to the back of her neck and was planting butterfly kisses on her skin, which made her shiver.

'Somehow it doesn't seem important anymore,' whispered Emma.

'Just wait until it rains again — it will then.'

'Of course, I've got a gap on the hall wall now . . . But somehow that doesn't seem to matter either.' She sighed happily and changed position in Chris's arms.

'Did you really come here in order to discuss interior design?' said Chris smiling down at her. Then his expression changed. 'Oh, I nearly forgot . . . '

'What?' asked Emma in alarm as Chris sprang away from her.

'The pictures. The ones you found in the loft. I came round to tell you, but then you started acting as though I was the worst thing since Jack the Ripper so — I didn't.'

'Tell me what?'

'The pictures you found in the loft,' said Chris going to the wall where various pictures were stacked. 'I've got them here somewhere . . . Not the one of the church. Ah, here it is — the one of the boats on the Yare. It's not a Cotman, but, by son of Cotman.'

Emma ran a hand over her by now disarrayed hair. 'You mean like 'Son of Sam'?'

'Yes, but in this case the son is an

artist not a mass murderer. John Sell Cotman was the father, the famous one, but Miles Edmund Cotman was his son and a well known artist in his own right! It's not worth an absolute fortune, but it should rattle up at least three thousand — if not more.'

'Wow,' said Emma. 'You said you thought that one was interesting, didn't you?'

'Well, I didn't want to get your hopes up, but I was pretty sure it was good quality,' said Chris modestly. 'I was going to give you till tomorrow and if you hadn't contacted me by then I was going to sell it and abscond with the loot.'

'You weren't — were you?'

'Not for a second,' answered Chris folding her into his arms again. 'How could I?'

'How could you what?'

'How could I leave without you, when . . . '

'When what?'

'When you . . . Wow — I've just got to say it . . . You take my breath away?'